Phoenix Academy: Col

CW01636988

Dear Master or Miss,

I congratulate you on your admission to Phoenix Academy. It is with great pleasure that I inform you of your acceptance and of the wide array of things you will learn at our wonderful academy.

Here at Phoenix Academy, set up by our very own Headmaster and King Magnus Phoenix, you will learn discipline, basic and advanced tactics, and so much more. You will be encouraged to discover your potential and you will learn how to be your best self under the teachings of the very greatest minds in the galaxy.

First-year subjects include, but are not limited to:

- Maths
- Science
- English
- Verantian
- History
- Engineering

- Basic tactics

You will also learn to use and develop the most up-to-date technologies and software, to crack the most complex of firewalls, and even to soar above the clouds in our very own student designed craft, the Warhawk.

We look forward to seeing you recruit.

#

"The start of something great is often the cause of something completely horrific. Many times in our history have children of warriors brought peace only to later be known as tyrants, such is the way of life."
– Valanor Escanovierten, *The Book of Tyranny*

Chapter One: The Class of 2220

In the galactic year of 2180 a great war broke out in the dark reaches of space. Three factions fought for control over the known galaxy, nearly destroying it in the process. The three sides that fought destroyed people and planets over an ideal, a fallacy. The ideal was self-importance, self-righteousness.

During what would become known as the Perpetual War many horrific acts were committed. I'm not just talking about the normal ones that soldiers have been doing since the great Vikings. I'm not talking about massive slaughter camps. And I'm not talking about the betrayal of one's own people upon their rescue. No. The Perpetual War was host to acts beyond the puny human minds capabilities of understanding. It was so horrific, so malevolent and so egregious that even the people who committed the acts and the people who had to write in great detail about them refused to think about or talk about or act upon what they know. Everything just goes forgotten, unspoken, lost. But not to me.

The war ended when the current King of the Verantians called a truce with the Emperor of the Imperium, after the largest battle in history, which was known as the Battle of the Devastated World. It took place above the ruins of the

Verantian homeworld and involved over ten thousand ships, including the flagships for each race.

Both the warlord Emperor of the Imperium and the warrior of honour King of Verantia perished in that battle, as the flagship of each society was caught in the ambush by Syndicate forces, who eventually fell to the advanced war weapons developed by the heir to all of Verantia.

The mantle of the fallen king was taken up by the new king, the well-known scientist Magnus Phoenix. Magnus, who had previously created weapons of war for the king, now crafted speeches of peace for his people. He vowed that if someone like him were ever to enter a position of power in the Imperium, Magnus would surrender and cost his people the war, in the name of peace.

Magnus didn't have to wait long to meet the man who would help him end the war. To be truthful, he met Xolistine the Second five days after his own coronation. Magnus had noted that he was "unsure" about the new Emperor and that only time would tell whether they would be able to end the war before one of the races was extinguished. However, only half an hour after meeting Xolistine the Second, he ended the war. Not because of anything Xolistine said, or a gesture to his forces. Not because Xolistine had a chance of winning. Magnus ended the war because Xolistine saw Magnus as an equal and extended his hand respectfully, in the way the Verantian people had done for hundreds of years when neither party were allies.

Xolistine seemed to care enough to end the war, and that was the only goal of meeting so soon after each had been crowned, so that they wouldn't have shed blood as rulers and wouldn't receive blame for any death during the war. The fact that Magnus was in pursuit of peace was evident during their short but fruitful talks. Peace not for him, but for future generations – for his daughters and sons, his grandchildren, his future great-grandchildren. Peace for those who were tired of fighting, peace for those that had fought. Peace for those that had died.

During the war, no propaganda had been required on either side. Most battles were recorded by surveillance ships or by actual combat vessels. To the Verantian people, it was a battle for freedom and equality, a battle to end slavery and to return the status of the Verantian people to a proud, strong, and united people.

For the Imperium it was a war of greed and of desire to expand and grow, but it was also a war of need. The need to preserve some sort of control in the galaxy at large, and to quash future rebellions before they happened.

No one had seen the hatred towards the Verantians coming – certainly not Magnus. However, after the war that hatred did come, and quickly. The third member of the war – the Syndicate, special forces for the Imperium – backed and partook in the genocide of the Verantian people and the destruction of all planets in the core owned by the Verantians – everything except the new Verantian homeworld.

The Verantian colonies that were too far from Verantia Prime to be hit by the Syndicate withdrew completely, separating from the monarchy. That left only one billion Verantian people under Magnus to rebuild the homeworld.

Once the war had finally ended, Magnus Phoenix started the organisation known as Phoenix Academy, and poured everything he had into the school. Using the wreckage of his homeworld and the wreckage of the ships he had designed, he made the city to house the school. He created a place for every one of every race.

As the school's reputation grew, so did its roster of students and its resources. It held the same amount of ammo and weapons as a large garrison, not to mention its research into new weaponry and the combined discoveries of both the Verantian people and the Imperials.

#

The year was now 2220 and Phoenix Academy had become

the biggest academy in the galaxy, sculpting the youth of today into the adults of tomorrow.

The Academy had many teachers, with four running the academy alongside Magnus Phoenix himself:

– His history teacher and head of security, Draxon Black.

– His daughter, the genius Eren Phoenix.

– His father and tactical educator, Aurelius Sivenestor, once an admiral with the great Verantian fleet.

– Science teacher and long-time experimental partner, Mr Crytal.

Much like when Magnus was a lad, the teachers were taken from all over the old Verantian territory and were each versed in different things. Some were pro soldiers, others mathematics geniuses and, of course, there was the Inventor King himself.

These teachers were awaiting the arrival of eighty shuttles filled with this year's students, and a single boy whose life would never be the same again.

#

Dean Ivanova, thirteen galactic years of age, awoke on the transport shuttle to Phoenix Academy. He and seventy other teenagers were being shipped off to the most critically acclaimed academy in the galaxy, and theirs was only the first shuttle of many.

Unlike the others, Dean had done everything he wanted from a young age. He had attended good schools and taken part in as many extra-curricular activities as possible. He had even helped around the farm by learning to repair the machines.

Dean looked around at the other students in the small room. The two boys, two girls and a Shé rén, were all spread out, each with their own bed and tablet.

The room was lined with shining white metal walls. There was no visible door. The floor was dark grey and made from metal grating with wires and pipes running below. The window, although it appeared thin, was eighteen millimetres thick and made from a transparent, aluminium alloy reinforced with thin lines of titanium.

Outside the window, Dean caught a glimpse of the red gas giant with yellow and orange swirls that seemed to chase each other and blend to make stunning lines of colour.

Dean had never seen space before. His eyes were filled with a want to learn and a want for the new life he'd signed up for.

It was a desire he put quickly to the back of his brain.

He watched as creatures flew past the window, creating minor turbulence that was quickly corrected.

His attention was drawn back to the pristine interior. All the floors and walls seemed new, but the window had slight scratches on it and the outside of the shuttle was covered in dents and burn marks.

All the students wore the identical white shirts, with black shoulders and button lining. The trousers were very light grey and their knee-high black boots reflected the light. The only exception was the Shé rén, who only wore a vest version of the shirt, his large, thick tail coiled below him.

The girl sitting across from Dean was writing on her tablet. She had red, shoulder-length hair and eyes, just like his. The second girl, who was asleep on her bed, was of Asian orientation. Her black hair covered her eyes as she slept. Glasses rested around her neck. Both girls appeared well built and healthy.

The boys were arm wrestling in the corner of the room. They had their shirts off and they were built like brick walls. One had blonde hair and green eyes, the other had blue hair and blue eyes. They stared at one another intensely, waiting for the other to give in.

The Shé rén was looking out the window at the passing stars. His white scales were tinted grey by black dots that peeked out as the scales aged.

Unlike his fellow cadets, Dean was messy with his

uniform, which was untucked. It suited him, with his short, messy hair and his red irises that glowed slightly. His hair was peat brown, and his eyebrows were perfectly trim and neat but natural.

He sat like someone ready for a fight, leaning forward slightly, one foot on the side of the bed to push off with and the other on the floor to support him.

Eventually, Dean looked down at his tablet. He placed his finger on the scanner at the bottom and it powered up to reveal a black background with a Phoenix emblem in the centre of the screen. The Phoenix was inside a golden ring, holding onto it with its talons. Its wings were spread, so that the tips touched the top of the ring. A golden spear pierced the top and bottom of the golden ring.

The tablet had three apps: a chat app that already had three notifications for him, a lessons app to help him with his scheduling and curriculum, and a map app. Each app had a part of the emblem as an icon.

Dean tapped the chat app icon. Three chats were open and two of them were updated every second. Dean deleted the two large groups, shaking his head in disappointment at himself as he did so. He imagined his brother saying, *You idiot. You're never going to make friends if you don't talk to anyone.*

Dean laughed. He thought back to the last time he had

seen him – but his thoughts were interrupted by a new notification that vibrated his tablet gently.

Dean looked down at the only chat he hadn't deleted. There was no name, only a number: 2212. He looked across at the red-haired girl, who waved before pointing to the tablet.

Dean entered the chat and read the messages 2212 had already sent.

Hey, what's your name?

And:

2213. What's your name?

Dean smiled and answered, *I'm Dean Ivanova. What's your name?* He looked up to see the red-haired girl smile and type something out.

His tablet buzzed again, but before Dean could check the message, the shuttle jerked, throwing him off his bed and onto the floor. He landed on his tablet. When he stood up, he discovered its screen was smashed.

Both girls appeared confused. The asian girl's red eyes were now barely visible under her hair. The Shé rén was looking around too, his tongue shooting out. He hadn't moved much, the sharp judder acting like a gentle stop to his strong-boned body.

As the human boys grabbed the shirts they had thrown to the floor, Dean came to a realisation. None of them had any luggage – it hadn't been brought aboard, instead left on the crowded station. He thought about his favourite book and his personal items.

Screams sounded from the hall, followed by a sound Dean knew all too well.

Gunshots rang from the hallway like bells in a deserted graveyard. Rounds bounced off the hull and the door as some small firearm unloaded into somebody next door.

Dean's instinct was to look at the Shé rén, who held up two fingers in the universal peace sign.

The screams died away followed by faint laughter. Dean saw fear in everyone's eyes. As he tightened his fist into a ball, a piece of his broken tablet in the palm of his hand made his hand bleed, and the pain made his arm shake.

Seconds passed in silence apart from the hiss of coolant leaking from a broken pipe in the hall. Suddenly, the door that blended in with the white wall slid open with a pressurised *whoosh*, and a man wearing a black and red uniform with an embroidered red cat emblem entered, holding a pistol.

"None of you move! This shuttle is now under the control of the Syndicate! Now hand me your tablets!" He held out a black rucksack in his free hand and everyone else except Dean put their tablets in. The red-haired girl looked at the floor as she deposited her tablet, along with the one belonging to the Asian girl, who was pretending to be asleep.

Louder gunshots sounded, causing everyone's ears to ring and the screams of students to weigh heavily on their minds.

The man, whose face was so pale he looked like the sun itself rejected him, looked straight at Dean. He smiled cruelly, his skin seeming to stretch and his yellow teeth reflecting white light, corrupting it.

"Now then," he said in a nasal voice. "What do we have here? You there, lad. Are you a Verantian?" He moved like a hunter who'd just seen his prey, stalking from left and right with quiet footsteps.

Dean nodded and approached the man with his tablet. As he got closer, the man raised his weapon. Dean froze. A sensation like a spider crawling made its way down his neck.

"I've got orders to kill all the Verantian scum I find. Lucky me." The man aimed the gun directly at Dean, who looked at the red-haired girl, who responded with an expression of desperation and fear.

Dean indicated to the other teenagers. "Before you kill me, will you at least let them close their eyes? I'd hate for them to watch me die."

The man shrugged. Fear crawled up Dean's body from

his tapping foot to his shaking, blood-covered hand.

"That's perfectly fine by me. Go on, children, close your eyes so I can pull the trigger." He grinned so wide it looked like his face might tear open.

Dean watched the red-haired girl close her eyes, then he closed his own, preparing to die. He thought back to his brother, sleeping on his lap at night.

BANG.

A gunshot tore through the room. Dean thought about his life, his mother, his disabled brother, the farm they lived upon before opening his eyes.

The man was dead. Blood seeped from the hole in his back, pooling around him and dripping through the grate. The bag of tablets lay on the floor.

Everyone else opened their eyes too. The invader was on the ground and there was a hole in the wall the size of a hornet. Something pitch black moved within it.

Blood had splattered all over Dean, from his face to his clothes, and even on the floor and wall behind him. He stood in shock, his foot still tapping gently and blood running from his shaking hand to drip into the growing pool of blood at his feet.

Another gun – larger, a rifle – appeared at the open door, followed by the man carrying it. The rifle itself had a long barrel with a large rectangular muzzle brake on the end. On the top was a large scope and on the side a smaller one clearly meant for close-range engagements.

The man wore full military gear: a black jumpsuit with black patches, a black plate carrier and dark grey elbow and kneepads. The carrier had shoulder protectors and a spinal mount to hold additional ammunition for the two pistols strapped to his thighs, and his polished black boots shone so much they could double as mirrors. He had black hair and red eyes, and his skin was damaged and scarred. His full beard was neatly trimmed and joined with his hair.

"You kids alright?" His voice was deep and relaxed. His expression was placid, as though he hadn't just taken a life or saved Dean's.

"Yes sir," Dean replied. "Although I was sure I was going to die..."

The others looked at him and the red-haired girl approached him. "Thank you, Dean... for the eyes thing. If he had seen my eyes, he would have wanted to kill me too." Her voice was shaky but calmed Dean. As she put her hand on his shoulder, the man at the door smiled.

"I need to press on and check the rest of the shuttle. But when I come back, I need to know everything, okay?" He waited until everyone nodded before moving along the corridor. His footsteps were silent; but the ringing of his gunshots reverberated.

"My name is Ellie, by the way. And thank you again." Ellie kissed Dean on the cheek before grabbing her tablet from the bag and typing furiously into it. She received messages back as quickly as she sent them, and seemed to be getting annoyed with whoever she was talking to.

Dean smiled and rubbed his cheek discreetly before returning to his bed with his cracked tablet. He watched the time tick by slowly. His only entertainment was the many chats blowing up, which he kept deleting, at risk to his fingers thanks to the shards of glass now sticking up from the screen of the tablet.

The Shé Rén had slithered into the corridor. After looking around, he returned with a pistol like the one the attacker had used. He looked it over, deep thoughts dragging him back to the window and the chaotic planet below them.

Hours passed before the man came back. His eyes were full of thoughts and his hands resting on the butt of his rifle, which was connected to him by a sling.

"Ellie, Dean, Ju Lan. Please follow me and mind your step. There are a few bodies in this corridor – I advise you keep your eyes up." With that, he continued walking. Something was hanging from his hand, but Dean was too focused on wiping the blood from his face to get a closer look.

Dean, Ellie and Ju Lan followed the soldier into the white-walled corridor. Ellie and the girl walked behind Dean, looking inside every room. There was blood everywhere. Ju Lan scanned her eyes over the cold, lifeless eyes of the dead.

In the hallway were many bodies belonging to both students and attackers. All the students had red, soulless eyes.

They walked to the end of the hallway and into a large room containing other men dressed like the first. They were finishing putting their gear on, and Dean noticed that one of them was wearing his plate carrier backwards.

The room didn't look too comfortable, but it had a gun safe and a cabinet full of plate carriers and utility belts. The chairs were simple and bolted to the floor crudely, and the table had a loose bolt. The soldier didn't seem to care. His equipment was clearly top of the line and from what little skin they could see, the three teens could tell he had seen battle and felt plenty of pain, as evidenced by the burns and scars covering his face and neck.

"Gregor. Jonathan," he said. "Scour the ship again and clean up the dead. Take the students to the infirmary and the infiltrators to storage." The others obeyed, leaving the room swiftly without reply. Their footsteps were louder than his, but still quiet.

"Excuse me, but what's going on?" Ellie asked.

The man smiled and took off his helmet, revealing messy hair just like Dean's. "Sorry, kids. My name is Draxon Black. I'm a teacher at Phoenix Academy. I also run the student security team, and the military units that make up our actual security. I woke up when I heard gunshots and... let's just leave it at that for now, yeah?" Draxon put his helmet on a table in the centre of the room, then added what had been his hand with a *clink*.

"Draxon. Are we safe?" Ellie's voice was full of confidence and her eyes were locked on the teacher's.

"So you're her, huh? I recognise your authoritative tone. Yes, you're safe. Unfortunately, you three are the only Verantians left." Draxon gestured to the chairs. When they had all sat down, he sighed.

"What's going on?" Dean had finally found his confidence. He didn't know why, but he was still scared. His hand was shaking, but he held it behind him. Both hands were drowning in his blood.

"It's alright, Mr Ivanova. I've dealt with the threat. As for what's going on, we were just attacked by the Syndicate." Draxon looked at Dean's arm, then at his red, shaking hand.

"We aren't anywhere near Syndicate space. What are they doing here?" Ju Lan was looking at the bodies in the hall as they were dragged away. One of the students had lost his boot in transit.

Draxon got up and closed the door, then moved to the window and gazed out of it. There weren't any ships in view and the sun was slightly to the right of them surrounded by nothing but blocks of barren rock and ice. The stars weren't the ones Dean knew, but wherever he was, he was better off than where he had come from.

"The Syndicate wants any and all Verantians dead, and they came here hoping to find some. I don't know how, but they managed to get aboard and kill twelve students. This is a failure on my part." Disappointment and hopelessness washed over his face. His muscles slackened.

"Commander Black. Phoenix Academy, dead ahead. Strap down for landing." The voice over the intercom seemed unaffected by recent events .

Draxon grabbed his helmet and sat down. The chairs automatically deployed belts to keep everyone locked down, and the remaining students were told to stay in their rooms and remain seated, until a staff member came to collect them, via an alert on the tablet. Dean's chair shook as they approached a large asteroid that seemed to come out of nowhere. As the shuttle passed a large metal door, the dancing of both the shuttles shields and the shields of the station made the vessel shake violently. The shuttle landed hard, producing a piercing scraping sound. Gently, the front of the shuttle tapped the wall of the hangar and stopped, its rear still hanging out of the large – but clearly not large enough – hangar.

When the belts retracted, Draxon stood and looked out the window. "Welcome to Phoenix Academy, kids," he said, his voice filled with relief. He left the room quickly.

Dean looked out the window at the metal box of a room. Hundreds of people ran around manically, some tending to different machines, some carrying large rockets on their shoulders. The entire room was a dark grey colour, except for the bright white symbol on the wall. It was a bright white phoenix with spread wings, a shield in its talons and a white circle stretching up to each tip of the wings and behind the shield. The circle looked like a planet, and it shimmered as Dean looked at it from different directions. The words underneath were written in old Verantian: *Dular engulf far unsaferna*. Dean smiled. It translated as: *Welcome to your gateway to the future.*

#

"Doorways go two ways. In order to let something in, you inevitably let something out. In the case of heroes and villains, if a great god ever existed, like our lesser gods, then he truly opened the door wide, for so much good in our society has been repaid with much suffering."

– Dolinor Caterslon, *The Book of Gods and Devils*

Chapter Two: Squad 212

The shuttle that had crashed in the hangar mostly consisted of a large engine and a long-connected interior. The flight controls were at the very front, accessed by a very simple pressure-sealed hatch. The outside of the shuttle was nowhere near as shiny as the inside, as it was that of an entirely different ship. The hangar wasn't much different, the equipment was all expensive and made intendedly for the large room, which appeared to have been built before the Perpetual War, before Verantia Prime fell.

Dean, Ellie, and Ju Lan disembarked with Draxon, ahead of the other students. They were immediately smuggled out of the large blue-grey hangar, which held hundreds of different small crafts, and straight into an elevator that looked like it had come straight from a horror movie – it had scratches and claw marks all over its walls and a little dried blood in the corner.

From the motion, Dean guessed they were going up. He looked at the girls, who didn't seem to be nervous, both standing nonchalantly, whereas his hand was still shaking and he hummed to fill the long silences. He could sense Draxon staring at him in the mirror and he could feel the cold breath of Ellie, who was standing unnecessarily close to him.

The elevator stopped and the door opened to reveal a bustling room filled with computers and screens, a holographic map, and a large window. This room was completely different to everything Dean had seen so far. The equipment appeared top of the line, the computers, and screens all brand new and the chairs wheeled and smooth as people pushed themselves from console to console. The walls here, too, were grey, though they shone brightly, and the symbol Dean had seen in the hangar was once more on display. It felt so strange to go from a place that was advanced yet simple to a room so busy, clean, and full of high-end tech that he feared letting blood drip from his hand onto the floor.

Looking out of the window was a brown-haired man in an outfit similar to Draxon's, except with a white collar with a golden pin on each side. This man stood on a slightly raised platform and he clearly demanded respect, but none of his men looked at him. In fact, even the cameras seemed to look away in fear. As Dean watched the back of this man's head he instantly felt... safe.

"Magnus. The survivors." Draxon handed his weapon and gear to another man, who took them away.

"Good job, Draxon. I knew something was up. Hopefully the Syndicate will think twice next time." Magnus turned around to look at the students. He was much like Draxon in how he carried himself and in how he kept a straight face however he differed due to his uniform and golden eyes. He did however hold his hands hidden behind his back and forced his legs to straighten even though he seemed to be weighed down by some heavy thoughts, carried by his broad shoulders.

"Your granddaughter was lucky. This boy here, Dean Ivanova, asked the assailant if the others could close their eyes. Quick thinking that saved their lives." Draxon stood behind Dean and put his hands on his shoulders.

Dean's nerves made him blurt out, "No... not really. I just didn't want her to watch me die, is all".

His statement caught the attention of everyone else in the room. Out of fifty people, there was only one set of red eyes. Dean's attempted light tone which obviously didn't sit very well. Dean could tell from the way the person closest to him moved the pictures of his wife and young daughter to the other side of the desk before turning them to face away from Dean, another fully shut down his workstation before moving across the room and setting up underneath a flickering yellow light.

Magnus's eyes had widened at the mention of Dean's name. After Dean's outburst, a smile grew on his face. It seemed the sort of smile a father might have for his son, or an uncle proud of his only nephew.

"It's okay, Dean. No need to be humble... But if I'm being honest, it really doesn't matter. In return for keeping my granddaughter safe, I would like you to accept private quarters and an automatic rank of cadet corporal." Magnus offered his hand and Dean shook it reluctantly, not having the confidence to decline or even to look him in the eyes.

Ellie reached behind Dean's back and grabbed his still shaking hand, making him freeze with fear as his blood-soaked hand, stained Ellie's perfect pale skin.

"Magnus," she said. "Mother told me you run a tight school. Yet your first action is to hand out a promotion and alienate Dean before the trials have even taken place?"

"Ellie, please. If you really think it's that big a deal..."

Ellie nodded.

"Fine..." Magnus let go of Dean's hand and sighed. Everyone else in the room turned away. Dean noticed a couple of the men handing the one with red eyes some small coins.

Dean was more focused on his hand, which had previously been bleeding but now was healed and clean. Ellie's hand was clean as well, as if she hadn't just held hands with Dean at all.

"Draxon. Is there anything you can think of that I can reward him with?"

Draxon nodded. "White collar status."

Across the room, someone dropped a ceramic cup. Everyone turned once more to look at the group.

"That should do," Ellie said.

It seemed to catch Magnus off guard. "Oh, so the highest award I can grant without a rank which leads to his own room anyway... This will alienate him more."

But Ellie and Draxon weren't budging. Dean's expression was one of shock and confusion.

The man with red eyes got up and handed the coins he'd just won to a woman who just entered the room, smiling. She dropped the coins into Draxon's hand behind his back.

Magnus chuckled. "Fine. I'll announce it tomorrow. For now... Ellie, can you show Dean to the private rooms whilst I speak with Draxon and Ju Lan?"

He waited for Ellie and Dean to leave, the elevator doors shutting with a slight suction of air.

#

Dean and Ellie were alone in the elevator as it went up. There was no music and Dean's cheeks flushed brightly from angst. He focused on the floor. Ellie watched him in the mirrored walls.

She cornered Dean. "I'm sorry about my grandfather. He's quite the people pleaser... but that's what you get when a king runs a school. Anyway, I'm sorry I lost you that promotion. You aren't mad, are you?"

He shook his head furiously, his face completely red, and held his hands in defence. "No, no, no! I would've preferred no reward... I'm not here for ranks." His voice was shaky and his left foot was tapping the floor.

"Oh? That's odd... Well then, why are you here?"

Instantly, Dean became depressed as memories flooded his mind. "I've come to do what my brother can't... He's paralysed from the waist down. He always wanted to be a soldier." Dean laughed a hollow laugh and kicked at the light layer of dust on the floor.

"Oh. That's admirable." Ellie let Dean move from the corner. "I look forward to you succeeding in your goal... but can I ask you something else?"

"Of course, feel free." Forgetting himself, Dean's smile was full of optimism.

"Wouldn't he be happier if you tried to rise through the ranks? I mean... if he could, don't you think he would?"

Dean considered this for a few minutes.

Ellie chuckled. His thinking pose reminded her of her grandfather's.

"I think you're right," he said, "but I don't see how I can raise my rank without help." He at the floor again.

Ellie kissed him on the cheek in a friendly manner. "You

have my help. Whenever you need it." She smiled as he once again turned red, his eyes and skin tone now matching.

The elevator came to a stop at the top of the facility. The doors opened to reveal twelve doors. Ten had name plates with ranks and titles and two had blank name plates.

"Here we are," Ellie said. "You're in that one on the right and I'm here, right next to my grandfather." She opened the door to her room, then waved goodbye before heading inside and shutting the door behind her.

Dean entered his own room. It contained a large double bed, empty shelves, a large closet, and a computer. The walls except those connected to the hallway and to Ellie's room were glass. Through them he could see stars and the blue and green gas giant the station orbited.

A knock at the door distracted him from the subtle beauty. When he answered it, the powered door opened with a rush of cold air.

Draxon stood in the corridor, holding a new tablet on top of a large metal box. "Magnus thought you might want some proper equipment, as we looked into your records... For what it's worth, I'm sorry. Anyway, I got you a new tablet. If you need anything, I'll be in the history room for most of the day, and otherwise I'll be on the range." Draxon slid the box inside the room, looking ever so slightly uncomfortable, then he left.

Dean put the tablet on the bed and opened the box. Inside was a full closet's worth of clothes – all the shirts with white collars – and even a fancy military hat, it was a peaked cap not unlike the hat worn by the United States Marines before Earth was absorbed into the Imperium's defence budget. There were six pairs of boots and shoes, all polished, and at the bottom of the box was a ceremonial knife and belt, as well as actual combat gear, all decorated with images of a golden Phoenix.

He looked around. It seemed strange to be standing in a room that felt more expensive than the shuttle he had arrived in, and it was far too large for a single person. He chuckled and his cheeks flushed as he remembered the one thing he had ever heard his uncle say before he disappeared looking for Dean's dad: "Son, when you grow up you'll quickly learn that you have a duty beyond want or needs. You hold the key to our race's survival. But that can wait." Dean smiled at his uncles's words before tapping his cheeks and looking in the mirrored computer screen, laughing at himself.

He put everything away, then had a shower and dressed in his new uniform. Then he sat against the wall in an empty corner of the room, and promptly fell asleep.

#

When he woke the next morning, four more ships were approaching the station. Dean turned to the door when it slid open.

"Dean, it's time for the trials." Draxon's eyes scanned the untouched sheets on Dean's bed before he looked at the young teen. "Did you even sleep last night?"

Dean nodded, then followed Draxon to the elevator.

"Draxon, sir..." he said, "what are the trials?"

Draxon who pulled out a small tablet. "Your trial today is... a written exam" He seemed completely disappointed. His face relaxed so much that he even started to yawn but stopped himself.

"So everyone does different trials based on when they arrive?"

Draxon shook his head. "Not quite. People designated for leadership roles are given easier challenges but the responsibility of a group of people. Luckily for you, you've been selected for leadership, along with your friends – not that I expected anything different from any of you. Put together, you three have better grades than my graduating year at the academy I attended when I was just a bit older than you are now."

Draxon stopped the lift a few floors below the command centre, letting Dean out before setting off again.

Dean walked down identical hallways, passing hundreds of doors. One room in particular called out to him, drawing him in. He opened the door just enough to see inside. What he saw turned him red. Pornographic media were taped to the walls. A young man a few years older than Dean scooted around on an office chair, his lab coat getting caught in the wheel and pulling him over as he moved.

Dean closed the door gently. He walked on, and eventually found his designated classroom, number 212.

A few people were waiting inside, including the young female teacher from the bridge, who wore a lab coat and was giggling at her mini tablet like a schoolgirl.

The desks looked aged, but the room seemed almost brand new. Dean sighed at the desk and chair combination. As he entered, he noticed Ellie and Ju Lan, as well as two others: a girl and boy. Both had pink hair and appeared almost identical.

"Look, Danny, another red eye. If our teacher wasn't golden-eyed, I'd have left by now," the girl said. She had a heavy Russian accent.

"Da. It's a shame freaks like that are allowed here," the boy – Danny – said. "Good thing they're not allowed back home, isn't it Danni?"

"Freak?" Dean said nonchalantly. "Wow... haven't been called that before. Get some original insults and I may get offended – but you're Earthlings, so that's unlikely."

A loud snigger came from Ellie.

When he realised what he had just said, Dean sat down at his desk with a panicked expression on his face. Ju Lan and Ellie were laughing to themselves and both Earthlings were looking at the three of them, eyes narrowed and full of hatred – though why that might be, Dean couldn't fathom.

The young teacher smiled. "Okay, now that everyone is here, you can all begin the test in front of you. No talking and, most importantly, no peeking." She tapped a small analog clock, which began to tick.

Dean picked up his pen and opened the test paper.

Question One: What drives you?

Dean smiled as he wrote his answer with confidence before moving on to the next question.

Question Two: Would you sacrifice others to make your dreams come true?

Dean's smile faded. He looked around at everyone writing away. The teacher noticed his anxiety. She looked at everyone else in turn before turning back to a panicked Dean. She made her way over and sat lightly on his desk. "Something wrong, Dean?"

"Miss... these questions... I don't know how to answer them. I've never thought about them and can't answer without thinking about them." He put his pen down in defeat.

"Is it something specific, or more general?"

Dean picked up the test paper. "General. None of these questions make sense... They're all so left field and odd. I mean what sort of question is 'Will you sacrifice others?' Who asks that?" He put the paper down again. Ellie and Ju Lan were looking at him, and the two Earthlings were laughing at their desks.

"Dean. I'd like to see you after class. Answer the questions you can, and once everyone else has gone, we'll work through it together." She smiled kindly before getting up from Dean's desk and returning to her own. "As for the rest of you, I suggest you ignore your surroundings and write your answers in full. Any peeking or conversations that aren't with me will result in immediate expulsion." The young teacher sat at her desk and watched eagle eyed as everyone resumed work.

Dean answered all but three questions: question two, question eight and question forty two.

Question eight: Would you rather save a school or a hospital in a combat scenario?

Question forty-two: Given the choice to have many wives or husbands, would you accept or stick with one?

He watched as Ellie and Ju Lan left the room chatting and laughing. Now he was left alone with the teacher. He knew the Earthlings were hanging around nearby; he could sense them listening in.

"So, Dean. Your trouble areas. Read me the questions." The teacher sat at the desk behind him and waited.

"Question two – would I sacrifice others for my dreams?" He stopped, looked down at the page, then put it down.

"What's wrong, Dean?" She moved to a crouching position next to him.

"My dreams... I don't know." He stopped speaking as she put her hand on his. She was extremely warm to the touch, as if a fire raged inside her.

"It's an open question. There are no wrong answers. These tests are to see what sort of character you have." She took his test paper and read through it.

"Miss, I—"

She put her hand up to stop him from speaking. "You're not a leader, Dean. You're a wolf, hiding amongst sheep. These answers are fake – I can tell just by skimming them. Do it again. This time, no thinking. Answer with your instincts."

She put a fresh test in front of him.

Dean finished the test very quickly this time, and when he put his pen down the teacher took the test paper from his desk.

"I see. I was right. Dean, I'm a councillor and a doctor in

many things. Your self-imprisonment isn't healthy. I'd like to know why you act so nice and why you do things for others before yourself, when in reality you're a smart realist with a dream of being a combat instructor." She put both tests in front of him and stared into his eyes.

"I just feel so guilty if I don't..." he replied. "When I was younger, my brother and I would go running. I was faster and I'd lap him, laughing the whole time. One day when we were running around the lake that we used as our course, I passed him and then I noticed some humans,. That wasn't a strange sight in itself, but they carried bats and bars and looked to be waiting for someone... Instead of slowing down to stay with my brother, I chose my ego and kept running. When I got back round the course, the men were gone... and my brother was lying on the ground. He'd been beaten black and blue, his breathing was painful and his eyes flooded with tears... It's all my fault..." Dean began to cry, but his eyes were no longer red, they were pitch black, as were his tears.

"Dean, look at me." The teacher snapped her fingers, drawing his attention to her golden eyes. "What happened was not your fault. It wasn't your brother's fault. It is the men who beat him black and blue who deserve to be suffering, not you!" Her tone had turned sour after hearing his story.

"That's another thing... My only dream was vengeance for my paralysed brother... and two years later, when I was running the loop, I got it" Dean looked straight into his teacher's eyes.

"You mean the men came back?" She looked away, as if the darkness in his eyes was too much for her.

"I saw them, and I made them suffer. I snapped every bone, twisted every muscle in their weak, frail bodies. Then... then I got them help, let them recover, and did it again – this time for myself. I killed them so easily, like crushing the heads of puppies." Dean felt himself slipping, so he bundled his fingers into a fist and punched himself.

The teacher saw his eyes fill with light red. She typed into her mini tablet, then put her hand on Dean's head and ruffled his untidy hair, holding him close to her, like a mother consoling a child.

Then Draxon entered the room. He and the teacher talked quietly in the corner. Dean's mind raced. *Expulsion,* he thought. *I've done it now,* he said to himself over and over. He started to well up at the prospect of a ruined future, a ruined life. Being a failure.

"Dean." Draxon approached and handed Dean a small white plastic card.

Dean looked it over, but there was no writing. "What's this?"

“A white card. A particularly high honour that teachers can give out when two or more teachers think it’s deserved.” Draxon put his arm around the teacher and pulled her into a side hug.

“Why are you giving this to me? All I did was answer some questions and lose my cool,” Dean said, tears clinging to his eyes as if for dear life.

“Because whilst you may still be confused and you may feel guilty... being here, facing humans and others that will judge what you did harshly? That takes some serious balls, Dean, some proper Verantian courage. You are everything this school is looking for in a student and everything I am looking for in a soldier.”

Draxon spoke with such gusto, such honest warmth, that the tears leapt from Dean’s eyes. “Can I hug one of you...?” he asked, looking at first the teacher and then Draxon, tears falling from his eyes in steady streams.

Draxon nodded and stepped forward. Dean rose from his chair and flung his arms around Draxon, crying into his plate carrier, which muffled the sound. Draxon looked at the teacher uncomfortably but she ruffled Dean’s hair with one hand and with the other patted Draxon’s back gently.

A little later, Dean left the classroom, his eyes dry and Draxon’s plate carrier soaked.

#

Dean made his way to the next class on his schedule. Science.

He sat as far away from Ellie and Ju Lan as he could. In fact, he sat away from everyone, on a table by himself. The teacher, a middle-aged man with half his face burned and his right eye covered by a metal eye patch attached to his skull by tiny bolts, not only focused on Dean's side of the room, but slowly made his way back as he asked questions – until it came to Dean.

"Excuse me young man – Dean, is it? Can you help me with this demonstration?"

Dean hadn't been listening at all and had completely missed the explanation.

"Yes sir." He stood up, still slightly glum after his test, and walked to the front of the class. Ellie was smiling at him, even though Ju Lan was still speaking to her.

"Right, Dean. What we are going to do is very simple. I am going to ask you to pour all of the ingredients into whichever flask you think is the most appropriate. If you are correct, you will receive points towards your final grade. If you are wrong, you will be taking a trip to the infirmary." The teacher took a couple steps back.

Dean looked at the three beakers before him, each of

which contained different liquids. He looked up at Ellie, who smiled at him and waved. Going slightly red in the cheeks, he looked at her again, this time through each of the beakers in turn. The first two were clearly glass, and Dean could see her well. The last one was a plastic polymer that wobbled when Dean poked it, and he was unable to see clearly through it.

Coming to a brash decision, Dean poured the contents of the glass beaker into the polymer one. Nothing happened.

"Well done, Dean, I'm glad to see one of us can see. I'll be honest with you, I knew which one was polymer, and I noticed the young princess staring at you from across the room. You need to pay as much attention to the universe around you as much the universe ahead of you. You can't get there without being here." The teacher looked at a now flustered and angry Ellie, then sent Dean back to his seat. There were mutters and even a few loud slaps handed out by Ellie, most of them to other girls making comments.

Dean smiled at Ellie and picked up his bag to move over to her. He spent the rest of the class with her and Ju Lan. The science teacher, Mr Crytal, laughed and joked with the students and spent what was left of the lesson mixing a cocktail of what looked like chemicals but turned out to be strong alcohols. When the bell rang, he downed it and sent everyone on their way.

#

The next class was Verantian language, which Dean spoke fluently, and his writing was perfect. Ellie, in contrast, could write it well but her pronunciation was off by a bit. Ju Lan was fresh to Verantian and couldn't read, write or even begin to pronounce it.

"Dean, how come you speak Verantian so well?" Ellie asked. "Most of the population don't speak it any more, and any that do are over five thousand years old. Surely you didn't learn it at home?"

Dean smiled and closed his notebook. "My first words were Verantian, the only card I've ever received from my father was written in old Verantian, and when my mum was too busy on the farm to look after me, this old woman would come look after me and my brother. She only spoke old Verantian." He corrected a couple of mistakes in Ju Lan's book. When Ju Lan reread it, she realised the dirty talk she had accidentally written originally.

#

After a twenty-minute was mathematics, with the teacher from that morning's test. Again, Dean was amazing. Ellie made a joke that his intelligence was that of an old man, but no one laughed. Ju Lan, however, made a joke about how he was likely a Syndicate spy, which everyone laughed at, even Dean.

The teacher was happy to see Dean finally settling in a bit, and she slipped Ellie and Dean each pieces of paper. What she said to Ellie turned her bright red and made her rush off to the restroom. What she said to Dean just made him smile and relax a bit. In old Verantian was written, *See, if you can talk to the princess like she's just another classmate, you can basically do anything.*

The next lesson was double tactics, studying simple battles from history that changed how battles were fought and how war was waged. Again, Dean seemed almost impossibly intelligent.

When his school grades were revealed, people stopped making jokes.

Dean had almost S rank skills in everything he had done, and he had reports from two other students who were noted as his only friends.

His reason for moving to the academy shook the class. People were shocked to hear that his brother was attacked, especially on their new homeworld, where criminal acts were so rare that a single prison could house every criminal on the large planet, and also double as a free hotel for those without jobs or a home.

Dean didn't let anyone discover his secret. Instead he brought attention to his extra-curricular activities, most notably the many school competitions in which he had won gold in every single activity he had taken part in.

Before people began to flock to him, he asked one question: "I never really like to talk about myself, but since I was surely just the example, who are we moving onto?"

No one spoke.

Ju Lan stood up and said loud and clear, "Cowards. My name is Ju Lan. I come from Earth – London, to be exact. My family are quite large but I'm the only one who wanted to leave that place. As I'm sure most of you are aware, I'm half Verantian, and that has played to my advantage. Due to most countries on Earth being friendly, thanks to the Governor, I've lived a well-educated, if not basic, life." She wasn't bothered about the two Earthlings staring her down from the back of the classroom, but when she turned to Ellie, she was shocked by her sigh of exhaustion.

"I guess I'm next," Ellie said. "As you all know, I am Ellie Maria Istania Oriana Myra Phoenix, a princess of the Verantian monarchy and a devout worshipper of the old Verantian gods. Unlike these other two, I was homeschooled, and manners were drummed into me like a second language. Luckily, I was allowed to attend the academy and give up any chance I had of actually becoming queen. Now, if any of you boys think I'm interested in you, then you are wrong. I've picked my man and I'll stick with my choice even if I regret it. My grandfather and his father were best friends and he is better than the person I was supposed to marry. Now, enough of that. Breathe a word of this to anyone and I'll kill you." She had begun mumbling towards the end of her speech, but when she threatened everyone she made sure they heard it.

The rest of the class remained silent.

#

"And the grand admiral approached the lonely goddess, his weapon raised and tears in his eyes. He did proclaim to that goddess he worshipped that for his people that he would forsake his faith, his skin and bones, his dreams of peace and family. That he would pay for all the sins of our race now and forever. Thus he became our god of suffering ELROC and he suffers even now for every crime, no matter how small."

– Archbishop Santoinosp Calicordianm IV, *The Last Reading at Supper*

Chapter Three: The Outbreak

Dean awoke the next day in his corner. He got up, dressed and put his white card in his shirt pocket, which he closed and tapped proudly. He put on his polished boots, picked up his tablet and left his room, and only then checked where he was supposed to be.

His new tablet had been slightly reinforced and had a nice rubber case to prevent damage. A couple of new apps had been installed on it, including an information app to look up friends and students, and it even had a teachers tab – though most of the information there was redacted.

The tablet had also been given a white-collar feature which meant that, unlike the others, he had full access to the app library, which contained everything from word searches to pornographic novels.

The first thing on Dean's schedule was the most important meal of the day: breakfast. As he still hadn't been to the cafeteria, he decided to use the map app, which crashed almost immediately. Dean chuckled in disbelief, before heading to the elevator, where he ran into Ellie, who was brushing her hair with a simple pocket comb.

"Morning," Dean said instinctively as he entered the elevator, still looking at his tablet. The map app closed every time he opened it, making him chuckle.

"Morning. Did my aunt help you with your test in the end?" Ellie was looking at herself in the elevator button panel, the scratches in the steel plate distorting her image.

"Yeah... Wait— your aunt!?" Dean smacked his tablet against the elevator wall, denting the wall and snapping the tablet.

"Jesus, dude, just how strong are you? And yes, my aunt. Gah you really don't know who our teachers are, do you?"

Dean shook his head in confusion.

"My aunt and Draxon are engaged to be wed. My aunt is a great inventor and designed the majority of this station and those tablets you keep breaking. Draxon is a great warrior and has led our armies and students from this school into battles without losing a single one. My grandfather is King of the Verantians and has the title of Grand Inventor in the Imperial court. As for everyone else, they either have done something of note for our society or are just very intelligent. Take our science teacher – he was one of the minds behind the slipspace engine."

Dean absorbed this information, then smiled. "Thank you, Ellie." He looked down at his broken tablet. Moments later, the elevator stopped.

"Now let's go get some food. There's plenty of time before lessons," Ellie said, dragging Dean out of the elevator, almost tripping on the broken doors as she did so.

Before they headed into the large hall, Dean dropped his snapped tablet off at the student help desk. The soldier at the desk was asleep with his feet up.

Inside the hall were thousands of students and hundreds of teachers. Many thousands of tables were set out.

Right at the centre of the room, trying to fight Draxon, were Danni and Danny. The Russian teens were trying their best, but Draxon was too fast and too agile. He always seemed to know where they were coming from. He pulled a baton out from his leg holster and hit both teens in the stomachs, forcing them to the floor, then held out his hands, satisfied in his victory.

"Anyone else care to give it a try?"

Dean looked around. No one, not even the older students, wanted to fight. It was clear that Draxon was respected and feared, but the two Earthlings seemed to have only been winded. The conclusion? Draxon had been massively holding back.

Ellie smiled and kissed Dean on the cheek as she pushed him into the circle. "Good luck!" She smiled and watched Draxon for his reaction.

"Ellie! Come on!" Dean looked around at the others before taking off his shirt and putting it on the table.

"Gonna try that hard, Dean?" Draxon smiled and put his baton away, casting his eyes over Dean like a hawk looking for prey in a field.

"No. Just don't want to ruin my shirt or break the card you gave me." Dean was in peak physical condition. For someone so young and skinny, he seemed to be less bone and more muscle. One way to describe him was that he was abnormally built, like a Greek statue or a Roman chest plate. His strength looked more fake than intimidating.

"That so?" Draxon smiled confidently and went to strike Dean.

Dean stepped to one side. He didn't throw an attack, but just defended and deflected Draxon's punches. At one point, Draxon closed in, trying to grab Dean but only managing to catch his wrist, which was game over.

Dean grabbed Draxon's baton and struck him under the chin, making him let go and stumble back. Draxon held his jaw, then clicked it and smiled. "Ow." As he looked up at Dean, his eyes changed from red to black.

They continued fighting into what would have been lesson time. Draxon was quick, but Dean was just as fast and used Draxon's own baton to deflect his hulking arms and fists.

"Enough!"

Magnus's voice silenced the rowdy crowd. Draxon's eyes snapped back to red. The students dispersed, returning to their seats and tables.

"Oops... you got me a bit fired up, kid." Draxon shook his head, then held out his hand for the baton, which Dean handed over before grabbing his shirt.

"Draxon... how many times must I ask you not to duel the students?" Magnus sounded disappointed, but unsurprised.

"Sorry, Magnus. What brings you down from the control room? Not this, I hope?" Draxon indicated the two winded students and Dean, who had just finished putting on his shirt.

"No. There's been an outbreak below. Fifth city this time. Take some Verantian troops and get down there to cleanse or cure it." Magnus looked worried and annoyed. He was wearing armour and carrying a pistol.

"Draxon, sir? What's happening?" As Dean approached, Magnus smiled, which Draxon noticed instantly.

"Magnus, no! I know I'll be short-handed but I'll just have to take some teachers. You promised we wouldn't drag students in on this one." Draxon stood between Dean and Magnus, reaching for his baton, his voice filled with anger.

"Draxon. You'll be outnumbered by millions. If you're lucky, this will be a basic outbreak. If not, you'll need help." Magnus put his hand on Draxon's shoulder. Draxon sighed, his hand moving up from his baton.

"They've barely begun training... They've had, what, a

week? You really expect them to not get in the way down there?"

Magnus looked straight at Dean. "Dean matched the worst upper-class man with a rifle –that's better than anyone else in his year. He also uses his instincts well. They've kept him alive so far. Ellie is smart and tough and is below Dean and three others with her shooting. Ju Lan may only be half Verantian but she's a wild fighter, and she's quick. Most importantly, she's a track sports champion on New Verantia Prime. Add in Danni, Danny and Asmodeus the Shé Rén and you've got yourself a decent reserve team," Magnus said reassuringly, his eyes locked on Dean but addressing Draxon.

"Fine. But only three students... no humans or anything else. Just Dean, Ellie and Ju Lan... If Ju will even be protected." Draxon walked away, rubbing his chin, defeated and bruised.

"Dean, Ellie – head to the armoury. Danny, Danni – find Ju Lan and send her to the armoury as well." Magnus walked out, ignoring the whispers.

Ellie and Dean left the room, hungry and confused. Shortly after they reached a large metal vault door, Draxon arrived with the inventor teacher, Eren, and Ju Lan. A few red-eyed, black-uniformed soldiers appeared as the vault began to open.

Draxon was first inside, handing out weapons to the eight soldiers and Eren before grabbing his own dedicated marksman rifle. He picked up three small versions of his kit and handed it to the students before taking three pistols and handing them over too.

"Ellie, Ju Lan, I'm giving you some small machine guns, known as SMGs. Don't muck around with them, especially after I hand you your ammo. Dean, I'm giving you a rifle like mine – we are a lot alike. So you'll stick with me unless ordered otherwise!" Draxon didn't wait for a response, handing Dean a rifle. He took a bag of extras from the shelf, then another bag of explosives, containing everything from grenades to a very large explosive charge.

"Draxon, what's my grandfather sending us into?" Ellie inspected her SMG, making sure it was sighted correctly and felt natural.

"Not here!" Draxon put the bag of extras on Dean's back before slinging the explosives onto his own back.

"Draxon, I don't feel comfortable bringing the students." Eren wasn't looking at Ellie or Ju Lan – her eyes were locked on Dean.

"He's killed before. His guilt will keep us alive." Draxon closed the vault after grabbing two large metal boxes, which he gave to another soldier.

Ellie and Ju Lan looked at Dean in surprise. Ashamed,

Dean looked at the floor.

They made their way at a run through the student-filled halls, Draxon shouting the whole time – "Out of the way! Clear the route to the drop pods!" – and pushing students aside.

When they reached a large, round room, Draxon opened the two large boxes and handed out several magazines of ammunition to each person.

"We can scavenge for more when we arrive if we need to. Eren, you take the girls. Travis, head for the fifth city and make sure not to leave the pod if you're surrounded. I have no idea what it's like down there." Draxon kissed Eren, who put her hand to his face.

"You're such a bad liar" she said with a smile. Then she led her group to a small pod which launched from the station, then was replaced by another pod.

"Lads, you head down next," Draxon said. "I'll take Dean alone. Stick together – and the same goes for you. If it's night, stay in the pod! Unlike Eren, you don't have golden eyes." He received a salute and a handshake from each soldier before they departed in their pod, which was quickly replaced by yet another.

Draxon took a moment to check his and Dean's gear. "Dean. You deserve to know what we're going into. You know how humans have a fascination with the undead?"

"Yeah. Vampires and zombies... it's kinda freaky what people come up with. I've watched all the old films." Dean helped load their pod with the extra gear and then secured it.

"The latter one... zombies. That's what we're up against. For some reason, this planet turns some people into the undead. Not everyone, but the rare few. And because it gets out of hand so quickly, we get called down to help the humans. We've conducted research, but we still don't know why it happens."

Draxon helped Dean strap in before strapping in himself and closing the door.

The pod was shot from the station and then plummeted towards the planet. To Dean's surprise, the ride was smooth, like a water zorbing exercise. Dean watched the humongous station get smaller and smaller until it was gone, covered by clouds.

"Sir... surely you're joking?" he said.

"No. Verantians are immune to whatever creates the undead, but they're worse than feral animals... I've seen men made of pure muscle who never so much as complained crumble and snap at the hands of these beasts." Draxon looked at the floor.

Beneath the clouds was a large dome with tracks leading to other domes. As the pod approached, a piece of the dome opened, allowing the pod inside but keeping the toxic gas outside.

The city within the dome was built like a megalopolis. From the large monorail to the smaller three-storey buildings on the outskirts, fires had been lit and humanoid creatures climbed over rubble in a monstrous manner.

The city was built in standard human design. It incorporated everything that was required for comfortable living, and its MKV habitation dome could support hundreds of thousands of people with very little risk and in increasingly dangerous planets and atmospheres. The MKV was built and designed by the Vertiri corporation on old Verantia Prime. With its downfall had come the downfall of many profitable and successful businesses.

Dean remembered reading about the dome and the fifth colony just after it was built when he was young. His mum had bought him a model, which he had glued over his light as a lampshade which made him laugh a little.

The pod decelerated rapidly, but as they passed a massive skyscraper, something hit it. When they passed another building, one of the thrusters knocked on the crumbling ruin, sending the pod careering into the largest skyscraper. It smashed directly into the glass and steel hotel, leaving a hole bigger than the pod itself. Rubble rained onto the streets below, hitting a few zombies.

Dean's eyes were closed and his hands still gripped the supports. Fear was still new to him. He didn't know how to use it, or if he even could, and that only made him more scared.

He opened his eyes, looking at the transparent roof, and through it the interior of a dimly lit room. Draxon was already unbuckling his weapon and Dean did the same.

Below their location, the city was in turmoil. A camp had been set up in a park, with scrap walls and gates, and people were hiding inside it as zombies ran into the wall, clawing, climbing, clambering, communicating with one another through screams and scratches.

Dean stood watching for a while. When the scrap gates caved in, he looked up at Draxon, who seemed about to speak, but then he swallowed whatever words he had prepared.

They both watched in horror as the clambering horde devoured the stubborn survivors. Yet again, humans were killing humans in ever more interesting ways.

The pod creaked and slid a little from its perch, but it didn't fall completely, leaning on another of its thrusters. In time that would crumble under the pressure, unless the building did first.

"Dean... we need to get out before the pod falls." Draxon unclipped himself and hoisted his bag onto his back. His tone was completely changed: he actually sounded scared. "Forget about the ammo. Just grab your bag and get in the room."

Dean obeyed. As Draxon opened the door, they both leapt from the pod, Dean pulling something heavy with him. A box of ammo had caught on his rifle strap.

The pod slipped from its lodged position and fell, smashing into a million tiny pieces, turning the zombies that had been ambling towards the tower into piles of glass, metal and flesh.

"Dean! I told you to leave the ammo. Doesn't matter now. Just turn around." Draxon spun Dean around and reached into the bag to pull out four items: two black tubes and two small flashlights. There were other things in the bag, and Dean was curious as to what they might be, but Draxon ordered forcefully, "Attach both of them to your rifle, then we can move out. They already cut power, even though they say there are likely survivors, and the security forces are keeping this place locked down. So this tower is going to be pitch black without any windows, and I want to get to the roof ASAP."

As he had been whispering, they had both attached the torches and the suppressors.

Draxon looked around the room, but then something fell past the window, attracting his attention. Two, then three, then four zombies fell past the window towards the concrete below.

Dean and Draxon looked out to see that the zombies that had been making a mess in the park were running toward the building as yet more zombies dropped from above, one actively trying to grab Dean on its way down.

As Dean stepped back from the edge, he saw opposite their position a four-propeller aircraft that had crashed into the building where they had lost their own thruster. Inside was a dead pilot, his missing parachute beside the door.

"Roof – now!" Draxon grabbed the ammo and led the way.

The hallways were empty except for luggage and blood stains. Draxon kept checking on Dean, and Dean kept checking behind him. As they went higher and higher, their pace slowed. Eventually they reached a staircase which had the red word *Roof* crossed out and replaced with *Hope*.

"Dean... whatever you see, whatever you do, do not make a sound." Draxon opened the door gently and they started up the narrow staircase.

Draxon shot three undead in the head before they reached a door that was propped open slightly with the handle of a machete. Gently, he put down the metal ammo box and moved closer to the door. He bent and picked up the machete.

When he got back to his feet, a rotted face smacked hard against the window, making both him and Dean jump back.

Draxon's foot knocked the ammo box, but Dean caught it before it made a sound. Draxon sighed with relief before shooting the zombie in the head and looking out the window.

On the roof, hanging from a piece of steel jutting from the side of the building, was a parachute. Something heavy was attached to its bottom.

"Dean, I think there's someone out there," Draxon said. "They're gonna need our help. I count maybe ten zombies that haven't fallen. Aim for the head."

Dean nodded, moving the ammo box out of the way.

Draxon opened the door as wide as it would go and together they emerged onto the roof, opening fire on the zombies. Dean took three or four shots for each of Draxon's.

When all ten zombies were dead, Draxon rushed to the edge of the roof and looked down. The man on the bottom of the parachute was already turned, but had no visible wounds.

"Dean, grab the ammo and then close the door." Then Draxon used the machete to cut the parachute, sending the man plummeting down.

Dean returned to the door and picked up the box of ammo. When he looked up, a pair of black eyes shone from of the darkness.

Slowly, a zombified dog emerged, and began to bark.

Dean pulled the ammo away quickly and slammed the door, scaring Draxon, who ran over and looked inside to see the dead, barking dog.

"That's new..." Draxon got level with the dog and shot two suppressed shots. One made a hole in the door and the other killed the dog. "I don't like the new."

Their victory was short-lived. Zombies started to pour into the open stairwell, all dead set on getting to the roof.

Draxon grabbed the ammo and blocked the door before pulling Dean out of view. Together, they held the door shut. Draxon reached for his radio, typing into it before returning it to his belt.

Dean looked at Draxon as he rested his full weight against the door. "What now?"

"We wait... till death takes us, or rescue arrives." Draxon turned both their lights off and rested his head gently against the door.

"Draxon... have you done this before?"

Draxon nodded before looking at Dean. "Only once... The only time I've actually feared for my life." He took off his helmet, then retrieved a snack bar from his pocket and began to eat it.

The daylight faded quickly, the hexagonal panels of the

dome simulating the day and night cycle with less ultraviolet radiation and thus less cancer, creating an eerily dark night with no moon or stars. It also began to rain, though Dean and Draxon were covered by the metal awning that clung to the stairwell.

Draxon sighed loudly.

Screams came from all over the city, along with gunfire. The second pod was visible, stuck on the spike of an antenna. All of Draxon's men were inside it, all dead. The water that filled the pod slowly was stained red with blood.

Report on the Fifth City

Magnus, I hate relying on you and your people for this, but another of the cities on the new test site has fallen to those creatures. Luckily we managed to catch it early and have cut off the water and power.

Unfortunately, because we acted so fast and our security sealed off the exits, letting no one who wasn't checked leave and no one enter, we've calculated that out of the four hundred thousand inhabitants, around two hundred and seventy thousand are trapped inside.

As of the time of writing this report, it has been three days. If it is anything like the first outbreak, then only about seventy thousand will be alive now, and if we don't act soon those numbers will drop, fast.

My security forces are still allowing some checked civilians through, but the numbers are lower with each passing hour.

The sewers are being used as shelter, but not even our security forces are willing to trap themselves down there to protect our people.

I know you lost half your men in the first city and have yet to fully replenish those numbers, but you and your people are the only ones who can resist this cursed plague on my colonies.

Whatever you need as payment, you need only ask.

With sincere regards,

President Vericules Eshatari

The Sovereign state of Moxcin

Protectorate of the Forx Confederacy

Owners and creators of the last human colonies

Last of the free human race

Chapter Four: The First Outbreak

Draxon cast his mind back a few years, to the first time Draxon and his peacekeeping force had come to the colonies. By the time they had realised just how bad it was, they had lost ten of their twenty squads, and the colony military forces had retreated to the main gates.

He recalled the first day he had experienced fear – the first day it had truly dawned on him just how little they knew.

#

Twenty years prior

A slightly younger Draxon sat atop a wrecked hover car, holding his rifle, and looking out over the city. The red car was parked on top of a large hill with a radio antenna that had been rigged with a black device.

To his left were a fake beach and ocean, and to his right a tall, red mountain range. The city comprised three clear sections: the beach resort, with a hotel spa with activities for anyone on holiday; the main living section, with small towers of flats and apartments and a monorail that snaked through the city that had now been destroyed; and the business area, which had a separate hotel that towered above the rest of the city and on top of it a VIP lounge called the Birdcage, where VIPs could hang out with other rich people and look down upon those less fortunate than them.

Draxon had been throwing stones as far as he could from his perch. A dust cloud snaked from the city in his direction, but for now he sat unconcerned and calm.

His head snapped around in response to the sound of footsteps, then jumped down from the car and ran as fast as he could from the edge of the dome all the way to the central, tallest tower.

The dust cloud had followed him, and the radio mast was no longer visible. One of the hexagons of the habitat dome had been broken by something.

Night had fallen by the time he reached the tower doors. Screams of pain and anguish sounded all around him as he pulled at the doors. The shutters on the inside were locked.

"Bastards! I came to help you!" Draxon cocked his rifle and turned to face the horde of undead running towards the tower.

"For... Aw, fuck" Draxon shot at zombie after zombie. The horde screamed and continued towards Draxon as he fired one magazine after another.

When over a hundred casings had hit the floor, the

horde stopped and turned in the direction of a new sound. A baby was crying in the distance.

The horde screamed louder as they turned to go kill the child, and whoever was unlucky enough to be with it.

"No... no! No! Hey! Over here! Hey!" Draxon banged his rifle against the doors, setting off the riot alarm.

The horde turned again, rushing once again at Draxon and the tower at great speed.

"Now you've done it," Draxon said to himself.

He let his rifle hang from its sling and took out his pistols, opening fire and reloading by dropping the magazines to the floor and reaching behind his back where his magazines were attached to the spine of his plate carrier.

As the first zombie reached him, Draxon was pulled backwards by something, dragged beneath the shutter. When the alarm shut off, he couldn't hear the baby anymore. He lay on his back, covered in sweat and breathing heavily, looking up at fellow soldiers in black.

"Idiot. Didn't you see the shutter was open enough for you to get in?" Eren said, looking down at him.

"Even if I did, I would never have risked crawling under it... Only a fool turns his back on a horde of hunger-crazed dead people." Draxon got to his feet. The dead were clawing at the riot gate as a soldier shut it fully, severing arms as the shutter hissed to a close.

"You've done it anyway. Thank you for last night. The time you bought us allowed us to restore power and secure the building." Eren held out her hand and Draxon sighed, then shook it.

"I'm here on the orders of our king, princess. It's by his will that you survive," Draxon clipped his rifle so it didn't hang so far, then returned his pistols to their holsters.

"If his will transcribes to your skill, then I would agree." Eren began to walk through the torn-apart building, past the military personnel standing guard at the shutter.

"Besides, it's a bit odd you thanking me for last night when you still haven't said anything about the night before," Draxon said, smiling cockily. "If I recall, you were quite speechless."

Eren bit her lip in annoyance. "I will admit that it was nice to be alone with you in a room away from the hissing pipes of the Academy – but it's nice to know you can't be trusted to keep personal and work relationships separate."

Draxon laughed. " I'm just glad you managed to lock down all the entrances." He took off his helmet and combed his hair with his fingers.

Eren stopped to look over her shoulder. "You mean both entrances."

Draxon stopped smiling. "All *six* entrances."

He turned and looked beyond the shutters. The horde was filing to the left and right, away from the shutter.

"Everybody, upstairs now!" Draxon cried. "Block the doors behind you. You two, with me." He grabbed two soldiers and led them through the reception door into the security office.

The passage into the maintenance tunnels was open. He heard screams from within.

"We close this hatch, and that closes four of six entrances. Then we have the garage and roof to seal."

As he and the men approached the hatch, they were pounced upon by undead, who dragged the unfortunate men to their deaths.

Draxon rushed over and slammed the hatch shut before toppling cabinets on top of it.

A scream from the main room told him it was too late.

Underneath the security desk was a shotgun. Draxon snatched it up and made his way into the main hall, which was now abandoned.

Carefully, he made his way to the garage and shut the shutter without issue. It was still night, and he could hear screams nearby, but he couldn't tell from where.

As he made his way towards the stairs, the door to the stairwell closed slowly. He rushed to follow whatever had just gone up the stairs but saw nothing.

He scanned each floor, finding only blood and carnage. All fresh. He made his way up the stairs, checking each floor, the shotgun held in front of him as he climbed the tower. Each room was filled with blood and bones, some bare and some with meat still clinging to them.

Eventually, he arrived at the hatch to the roof, where the bodies of zombies and humans lay in piles all the way to a blood-covered ladder.

The whole time, Draxon had thought he was being watched, but each time he checked his six it was clear. Sometimes he had spotted doors moving silently, but nevertheless he was sure he was alone.

He checked the hatch and ladder for traps. When he was satisfied, he laid the shotgun against the ladder and climbed up.

As he cracked open the hatch he was blinded by light, and woke to a bright, rising sun. He looked around to check if he was really awake and smiled to find himself safe.

Dean was asleep next to him, on the other side of the door, which was now ajar. The ammo box was missing, as was the machete.

Draxon looked around, trying to find something – anything – that might give him hope.

What he saw only freaked him out more. The second team had been beset by thousands of zombies that had climbed up the building and into their pod in the night. Now the horde of dead humans were eating his men, and he was unable to do anything or even to move from his position.

Footprints on the roof had dried after the rain. Someone had been walking around.

Draxon checked his weapons. One of his pistols was missing, along with a few magazines.

He had no clue how, but they had been robbed. Surely he hadn't let his guard down that much?

Surely he hadn't failed Dean like that.

#

"The concept of reanimation is nigh on preposterous, yet we readily accept the theory of reincarnation. If one is possible, the other must be plausible."

– Dr Aventoru Denifortruo, *A Science of the Mind*

Chapter Five: Fifth City

Dean woke to Draxon sweating hard. Dean noticed the door was ajar, and through it he could see something Draxon couldn't, at the top of the stairs in the corner.

Small.

Fat.

Hungry.

Panicking, Dean jumped to his feet, moving away from the door. The baby zombie came crawling out with its umbilical cord still attached.

It chased after Dean, but before it got far onto the roof, Draxon crushed its head with his boot. He grabbed his rifle, stood up and closed the door, then walking over to Dean, checking him for wounds. Dena was breathless and chocked at the whole series of events, he even tried to push Draxon away until the shock wore off.

The night before, they hadn't noticed that the door was covered in scratch marks and bite marks, as if the zombies had been trying to get in.

"Good... you're not hurt" Draxon sighed with relief.

He looked at the door in response to sounds of gunfire. The door burst open and Eren, Ellie and Ju Lan came through, slamming it shut behind them.

"Eren, finally. Me and Dean—"

Eren cut him off, throwing her arms around him. For a while, she simply wept.

"My lord... Eren – what's wrong?" Draxon asked, looking into her golden eyes.

Eren tried to hold back her tears. "It affects us! The virus, or whatever took Travis! He died defending us."

Draxon pulled Eren in close and hugged her.

Dean made his way over to Ellie and Ju Lan. Ellie had vomit all down her plate carrier and Ju Lan looked sickly too.

"Are you guys doing okay?" he asked as he sat down. He took one of each of their hands and held them tightly.

Ellie looked at her boots and sighed. "I'm fine, but Ju Lan is struggling. She watched Travis... Well, she had the front seat view."

"Ju? Do you need anything?" Dean shook Ju Lan's hand gently to get her attention. She looked spaced out. She shook her head before reaching for her water bottle, which was empty.

"Here. Have mine – as much as you need." Dean handed her his bottle and she took it, drinking its contents.

"Draxon – something is wrong with Ju Lan..." Eren said. "She and Travis both drank water from one of the fountains... but I thought the water was turned off like the rest?"

Draxon looked at Ju Lan. She had passed the bottle back to Dean, and he was about to drink from it.

Draxon ran over and took the bottle, then threw it from the rooftop. It spun through the air, emptying water everywhere, and eventually it hit a car at the bottom of the tower with a smash as it broke the window.

"What the hell!?" Dean exclaimed.

Draxon pulled him away from the girls. Addressing Eren, he said, "Did you touch the water, or the vomit?"

Eren shook her head. "I've been protecting them since Travis. Haven't stopped all night. These ones don't care about time of day either." Eren fell silent, checking her last magazine.

"Eren… think back to our last outbreak. The water. Everyone who turned drank it, someone did something to the water."

Ellie and Ju Lan looked at one another – then Ju fell to the floor.

"That said, we'd need to purge them of both fluids… but Ellie never drank anything." Eren looked at the vomit, then at Draxon.

Dean went to approach them but Draxon held him tight.

"We can't just alienate them…" Dean cried, "and we can't let them die!"

"We won't let them die… but we need this tower to be

safe. That means shutters down. Tunnel locked. Roof access only." Draxon reached for his radio and began to type into it.

Dean watched him for a few seconds, then asked, "Why don't you just speak?"

Draxon shook his head. "If they hear the fear in my voice, they won't come." He sent the message.

Dean pushed away from Draxon's grip and ran past the girls, then down the stairs to the shutters at the bottom floor. He'd avoided zombies by sticking to the shadows and not making sound, although there weren't many zombies at all now, in contrast to the point when the girls had arrived.

At the bottom of the stairwell he slowed, peeking around corners. Cautiously, he approached the control panel for the main doors and made sure the doors were shut before dropping the riot shutters.

As they clattered to the floor, he heard screaming from inside the hotel.

Then he heard something he didn't want to hear.

A siren.

He rushed to close the other shutter, but it was too late. The riot alarm had gone off and the horde was approaching rapidly.

Dean ran into the office and slammed the hatch, then dropped anything he could find on top of it before heading to the garage.

No good.

A hover car had crashed into the wall, directly below where the shutter ought to close. He tried moving it, but he wasn't strong enough. Panicking, he lowered the gate as low as it would go before he turned to face a group of zombies.

He unloaded his rifle into them, emptying his magazine. He reloaded and ran for the stairs, but as he looked up the single stairwell he saw hundreds of zombies blocking his path. Some of them were already heading down.

"Shit, fuck, crap... Stupid, stupid, stupid!"

The elevator doors were open, but the power was off. He would have to climb.

He rushed to the elevator shaft and started to climb, reaching the third floor before realising how hard this was going to be.

Finding an open set of doors, he tucked his plate carrier, heavy equipment, and the bag of ammo behind a bench before setting off at a brisk pace, his only armour his helmet.

"Idiot," he said to himself. "Should have just waited for Draxon."

He climbed and climbed, even after his arms tired, eventually stopping at the fifteenth floor. He checked the stairwell. It was only filling up more.

In a moment of pure idiocy, beyond what he thought himself capable of, he returned to the shaft and began to climb even higher.

After reaching the twentieth floor, he checked the stairwell again, this time out of pure need.

The lift was stuck at the floor above, and he wouldn't be able to get past it. He jumped into the stairwell and ascended two floors, only to find the door to the main floor blocked. He tried the next floor, but that too was blocked.

Dean realised he was now trapped. Zombies had cut off the floors below, and the stairs ahead were also filled with zombies.

"Give me a break," Dean sighed. He doubled over to catch his breath.

When he leant on the door leading from the stairwell to the twenty-fifth floor, he fell to the floor. He closed the door quickly and leant against it to hold it shut.

In front of him, hiding under a bed in a room he had checked the day before, was a young girl. Her right eye was black, and her left eye was covered by a bandage.

Dean looked around before getting up and approaching her.

"Hey? Is it cool if I hide with you?" he said. "It's just that I don't want to be alone."

When she nodded, he slid beneath the bed, having to bend his legs to fit into the small space.

They waited for a few hours, during which time the zombies walked up and down the stairs, until at last they went down and didn't come back up.

Dean emerged from under the bed, then helped the girl out. She was around eight and only went up to his shoulders, the hood of her pink coat adding to her height. Her shoes flashed when she walked, which made Dean nervous.

"My name is Dean. I'm going to need you to stay real close, okay?" He smiled at her.

She smiled back, then grabbed his hand. He hesitated before leading her out of the room and up the stairs. As they left Dean looked back into the room to see what he assumed to be her parents, sitting down on the sofa as though watching TV.

"Are those your parents?"

In response, the girl drew her finger across her throat.

Dean shot the few zombies they encountered before moving on. When they reached the door, he banged on it.

"Draxon. Eren. Guys."

The door opened and Draxon dragged him onto the roof, along with the girl, crying, "You moron!" He punched Dean, knocking him to the floor.

"Draxon! I closed the shutters! The garage one has a car blocking it, but they're closed... We can call for help and save my friends now, right?" Dean held his injured nose with one hand. The girl was still holding his other hand.

"Yes... we can. Who is this girl and where's your gear?"

After Dean told him everything, Draxon helped him up. "That riot alarm probably went off because of the car," he said. "The thing that troubles me is that we already cleared the floors – so how did we miss them, let alone her?" He gestured at the girl.

"Draxon... where are Ju Lan and Ellie? And what about Eren?" Dean looked around to find Ellie and Ju Lan handcuffed to a rail at the side of the building. Eren was injecting them with a large syringe filled with a cloudy solution.

"Eren has sedated them. They'll need all their strength to resist this parasite... a disease is too unlikely. I've told Magnus – he's sending a quarantine crew as well as food and water... and guards... students too... against my advice".

The girl hugged Dean's waist tightly. "Big brother... I'm hungry..."

Draxon chuckled, then handed her a bar of chocolate from his plate carrier. "Here ya go, little one. If you need water, you only have to ask." He smiled as the girl took the chocolate and started nibbling.

"I could've done with water," Dean said under his breath.

The dome opened up to reveal a cloudy sky with trails of dust and debris plummeting towards them. A few more pods broke through the dome, landing in areas surrounding the tower.

Draxon tapped Dean on the shoulder. "Alright, kid... this time you stay here. I'm going down to get our guys. If zombies make it up those stairs and out here, it's game over... Do what you have to." He didn't give Dean time to answer, and within moments he was through the door and down the stairs. Dean was too tired to go after him.

Eren smiled at Dean as she stepped away from the girls. "If you really need to, you can always just ask to talk." She glanced at the small girl, who was asleep, the remaining half of the chocolate bar still in her hand.

Dean slumped against the door. "Talk? We're supposed to be soldiers – and yet the first thing I do, the first thing that really felt right... was wrong."

"Dean... Draxon went to look for you when the alarm started... but the zombies piled in from somewhere and he was stuck here. But he and I had a chat. Given that you made it back, you did the right thing. It's if you *don't* make it back then you know you did the wrong thing."

She put her hand on Dean's shoulder. The same moment it made contact, Ju Lan began to convulse and foam up at the mouth. Her body contorted in ways that broke her bones, and the foam poured out from her mouth like froth on beer.

"Fuck! Dean, gimme a hand. Put some gloves on!" Eren ran over and uncuffed Ju Lan from the wall, then slipped a large red pill into the young teen's mouth and forced her to swallow. It stopped the foam but not the fit.

Dean put on a pair of white latex gloves and knelt next to Eren. "What do I do?"

"I need you to make her throw up," Eren said as she began mixing something in a small bottle.

"What? How?" Dean looked at Ju Lan, then at Ellie, who put her fingers in her mouth as an illustration.

"You want me to make her gag it up?"

Both Ellie and Eren nodded.

Quickly, Dean forced two fingers through the foam and all the way to the back of Ju Lan's throat. Seconds later, she was vomiting. The vomit dissolved the foam and cleared her throat.

"Now make her drink this!" Eren handed Dean the vial, and he forced Ju Lan to drink it.

She awoke a few seconds later, but her eyes were strained

and wild.

Eren cuffed the girl to the railings once again, then pulled Dean away before Ju Lan could bite him. Then she ran to the front of the building and looked down at several men who were building a barricade from vehicles and scrap. "Fuck!" she cried.

Draxon's voice came over the radio. "Eren. I'm on my way up with the quarantine staff. How's Ju Lan?"

"She's... devolved. Draxon – the parasite... if it causes devolution or evolution, it could be of use." Eren turned to look at Dean, who was between Ellie and Ju Lan, trying to keep them apart. Ellie's eyes glowed golden.

Eren ran over to them, but it was too late. Dean's eyes turned black and he headbutted Ellie, knocking her out.

Ju Lan jumped back, trying to get away from Dean, tugging at her cuffs with all her strength.

Dean had Ju Lan by the collar of her uniform. She was clearly terrified. Eren went to pull him off, but his grip was firmer than a statue's. He lifted Ju Lan up, despite her hand still being cuffed to the railing.

Then he dropped her.

Draxon emerged onto the roof just in time to witness Dean collapse against the side of the building, clutching his head.

"Dean, take it easy! What happened?" Draxon ran over

and looked at Dean, whose eyes were shifting uncontrollably between black and silver.

Dean rubbed the red mark on his forehead. "My head... Ellie... I hit her."

"Alright, Dean," Draxon said, his voice full of worry and shame. "You sit here. I'll get someone to give you something for the pain." He rose and went to Eren.

Seconds later, Dean fell unconscious. The last thing he saw was Draxon walking away, a few dog tags hanging from his hand.

#

"Expecting others to die for your cause is the job of a general. Though no general truly understands the consequences of his orders until they are thrust upon him."

– High King Sylvester S. Sortovenic, *A King Written Up*, Ustinover Colinortink

Chapter Six: Consequence

When he awoke, Dean found himself lying on a large bed with Ellie next to him and Ju Lan asleep on the floor. Slowly, he slipped out of the bed and through the door, taking his rifle from a drawer as he left.

Draxon was sitting on the bench outside the room. Eren and the young girl were playing pat-a-cake beside the large window overlooking the city.

"Draxon?" Dean clipped his rifle on and approached him.

"Ah, Dean. You're finally awake. The other students Magnus was sending are awaiting command. I want you to come with me."

Draxon and Dean slipped downstairs without the others seeing, going all the way to the ground floor.

The hotel had been cleaned up a lot, and survivors were arriving in their hundreds. The soldiers that had come down from the academy were slightly different to Draxon: they mainly consisted of mixed races, some with horns, some with scales, but all tough-looking making Dean finally feel like he could release some stress – until he saw the cadets.

Danny and Danni, as well as the Shé rén and twenty others, were standing around talking in groups. The Shé rén was looking out of the window at the heavily manned barricade.

Draxon raised his voice to catch their attention. "Cadets!"

Quickly, they moved into a parade formation, five abreast and five back, and waited for their orders. Each of them was carrying a short rifle with a torch and foregrip.

"Cadets, I won't lie to you. This trial is the cruellest I've seen at this Academy. If it were my decision, you would be on the station and as far away from this as possible. That said, it's not my decision. However, what you *do* is my decision. Danni, Danny and Shé rén, I want you three to follow young Dean and his friends downstairs and clear the tunnels. Seal all access routes before coming back here and resealing the security office entrance." He tapped Dean on the back, as Dean was mid-stretch and yawning.

"That's stupid!" someone said.

"I'm not following that scum!"

"You will do as ordered!" Draxon shouted, making Dean to grab his rifle faster than he would have thought possible.

The door to the stairwell was held open by a fire extinguisher due to the arm at the top being busted as the zombies broke free from the confines of the stairwell the night Dean and Draxon slept on the roof. Around the room, medics were tending to people, all of whom became scared when Draxon shouted.

"Draxon, I'd appreciate it if you could relax," Eren said.

She and the girls had come out of the stairwell and now she stood behind Dean, letting him relax by placing her hand gently on his shoulder.

"Shouting will only endanger us."

Ju Lan wore around her neck a black and gold collar with an electric leash, much to the discomfort of everyone in the room.

"Is the leash really necessary?" Dean asked.

Eren nodded. "With the devolution, she's more like a wolf or a hound than a person. She'll fight better than any human could, though, and won't retreat unless she feels her survival is threatened. I don't really want to send her with you, but she's afraid of you and that means she'll listen to you." She handed the leash to Dean.

Ju Lan walked like normal, but her eyes were bloodshot and her teeth were sharp like fangs.

"Right..." Dean said uncertainly.

Ellie pulled her helmet down over the red mark on her head, her golden eyes full of shame.

"As for the parasite," Eren said, "it can't negatively affect you three, so—"

She didn't get to finish her sentence. Danni shouted,

"*Negatively affect?* What the hell would you call that, then?"

Dean pushed through the people standing in front of Danni and covered her mouth as he forced her to the floor, his eyes black.

"Shut up!" he hissed. "If you shout any louder, we won't have to go hunting! The Zs will come to us... you don't want that."

He was thrown off Danni by Danny, but then Dean pointed his rifle at the boy and everything became very heated causing the entire group of cadets to choose sides that quickly became confused. Both Danny and Danni pointed their rifles at Dean, who aimed his rifle at Danny, his finger inching closer to the trigger.

"Enough," Draxon said, pulling Dean out of the mess of cadets and hitting the back of his head hard enough to calm him down. "For the sake of the king, *enough*. Dean is in command of your squad. He is the only one I trust, and since he nearly got himself killed yesterday, he knows when to retreat."

Now everyone was quiet, apart from Ju Lan, who growled at Danni. Her eyes followed him, only stopping when Dean came between them.

"Do you intend to argue?" Draxon pulled hard on Ju Lan's leash, making her whimper like an injured pup.

"No sir," Danni and Danny said at the same time, saluting as they did so. They spoke through gritted teeth, anger sitting at the back of their throats like a lodged candy.

Draxon looked at Dean. "What about you, Dean? Any issues following through?"

Dean shook his head. "None, Draxon. We'll get the job done."

He walked away with Ellie and Ju Lan, followed by the other three, the Shé rén bringing up the rear.

As Draxon watched them leave, he muttered under his breath, "He should be calling me sir." Then he looked at the other cadets and sighed.

Dean and the others entered the security office with Eren, who helped them move the two desks and three cabinets Dean had thrown on top of the hatch in a rush.

"Dean, these are bloody heavy," she said. "How did you move them alone?"

Dean rubbed the back of his neck. "I don't know." Then he added, "Who put me in the bed with the girls?" He only realised what he had said when Danni and Danny laughed.

"I did," Eren replied. "You were as cold as ice and you needed to be warmed up. Ellie was feverish and she needed to cool down, so I issued a doctor's note and put you side by side in bed. With Ju Lan as your guard dog."

As she lifted the last desk, the hatch burst open. A zombie lurched out, heading for the twins, who had only just lifted their weapons when the zombie fell dead at their feet, courtesy of Eren's custom pistol.

Dean looked down the hatch and turned on his torch. "Rifles up, you two. You're our ladder guards."

Ellie peered into the red-lit tunnel. The only thing visible at the bottom of the ladder was a pool of blood. "Dean... there are a lot of pipes down there. Are bullets a good idea?"

"You have a point. Knives and batons it is." Dean clipped his rifle up and took an extendable baton from his belt.

Ellie did the same, handing her knife to Ju Lan, who hugged her and kissed her on the cheek.

"No guns? You have got to be kidding me!" Danny gestured at the dead zombie which looked like it had once been a security guard or at least someone with a very similar uniform, its white shirt covered in blood and bile. The black trousers torn and tainted with the stench of death.

Eren rested her fingers on her chin much like her father did and sat down in a swivel chair. "No, Ellie was right to bring it up. If you break one of the pipes, you could alert all the zombies down there and cause a miniature horde... trapping and killing you."

Dean and Ju Lan went down first, Dean giving her his knife as she reached the bottom of the ladder. She kissed him on the cheek as she had done with Ellie, then looked around, sniffing the foul, damp air.

Ellie, Danni and Danny followed next, the two Russians still using their rifles Dean not bothering to make a fuss as to not attract and zombies that might be close by. The Shé rén was the last one down, and he closed the hatch behind him.

The maintenance tunnels were cramped, with barely enough space for two people to walk side by side, let alone run. The red light made it seem as if the wet walls were covered in blood. Pipes and wires ran along the damp walls, some of which had been cut and some bitten into. No rats scurried along the concrete floor, and no roaches nor bugs of any kind, not even spiders. Yet a breeze coming from both directions made the tunnel feel alive. Ellie shivered as her boots made contact with a blood-filled puddle, the sound echoing.

"Dean. Which way first?"

Dean looked in both directions. "We'll split up. You take that way with the twins, and I'll head this way with Ju Lan and the Shé rén. If you need help, tap your radio button twice. When you completely closed any entrances to the tunnel, come straight back here."

Within moments, Dean had passed around the corner with his group. With every step the group took, the sounds of dripping water became louder. Soon they came across the body of a dead maintenance man. Next to him was a toolkit. One of the pipes was loose, letting drips of water drip and drip and drip.

"Dean... that's your name, right?" The Shé rén slithered quietly behind Dean, who walked behind Ju Lan. She was sniffing the air like a hound tracking a scent.

"Yeah. How would you like me to refer to you? I always thought Shé rén was your race, or at least that is what I learned in school." Dean slowed in response to Ju Lan slowing.

"The man who found me called me Asmodeus, but most people call me Shé rén out of respect for my rareness... or 'scum', if they're from Earth." He took a machete from the sheath on his back.

"Asmodeus? It's a good name... better than Dean. Hang on." Dean crouched behind the wall and looked round the corner, where Ju Lan had halted and was rubbing her nose.

Eight zombies stood in a circle, all looking at a Verantian soldier who appeared to be struggling to breathe through a heavily bleeding throat.

Dean unclipped his rifle and laid on his side, still watching the circle of undead men. He shot six times, killing all eight. Each of his .308 calibre rifle rounds was more than powerful enough to pierce two rotten heads.

"I thought you said no guns?" Asmodeus said.

Dean stood up and clipped his rifle up again. "I did... but I also don't plan on ending up like him." His eyes turned a dim silver as he pointed at the dead soldier.

"Makes sense." Asmodeus slithered over and inspected the corpse.

They had two possible routes. One would involve doubling back on themselves via another tunnel, but the other would head straight outside into a zombie-filled car park. More fresh corpses lay not far from the door.

"Ju, I need you and Asmodeus to check round that corner for me." Dean handed the electric leash to Asmodeus, who looked at it uncomfortably.

"What are you doing?" Asmodeus asked Dean.

"I'm going to lock that service entrance. I just don't want to be jumped from behind." Dean unclipped his rifle and approached the large metal door at a fast walk.

When he looked back, the others had already vanished around the corridor. Dean smiled and began to close the door. It scraped loudly against the floor, attracting the attention of zombies in the garage, and more outside.

He pulled the door with all his strength, and it closed and locked moments before the first zombie reached him. Dean laughed as they banged against the door. He was sweating heavily, partly from his exertions and partly due to the stuffy, dust-filled air.

The door was red with rust and had the words *Foreman's Office* crossed out and replaced with *Garage*.

Asmodeus and Ju Lan came around the corner. They were covered in dust and blood dripped from Ju Lan's knives as she walked.

"No need to worry about that direction from this side," Asmodeus said. "Cave-in. Might be worse on the other side, but we should check on the others."

The radio clicked twice. Both times, the twins could be heard shouting, along with the screams of zombies.

"Ellie!" Dean sprinted away from the other two, picking up the dead soldier's light machine gun along with his bag as he passed.

He cocked the LMG as he approached the ladder. He rounded the two final corners at speed, his rifle swinging at his hip.

Screams pierced his ears as he got closer.

As he turned the final corner, he saw that the door was closed, but both twins were on the floor being devoured. Ellie was holding off a few zombies with a piece of piping, her baton snapped in two on the floor.

Dean unloaded bullets into the zombies, then looked along the corridor to his left to see the light from the cave-in and the shadows of more zombies approaching. He switched his position and shot the remaining rounds within the LMG, taking out a few zombies.

Ellie hugged him as he helped her up. "Dean! Oh my god, I thought I was dead!" She kissed his cheek.

He smiled, pulling her around the corner, away from the cave-in. "I came running the second I heard the two clicks. We should get back to Draxon."

He heard groans, and he turned his head to see the twins rising from pools of their own blood. They were staring directly at Dean, as if their hate for him had followed them into the afterlife.

"Ellie, run!" Dean pushed Ellie and followed behind her, leading the two corpses back to the ladder.

Asmodeus and Ju Lan were waiting for them. As soon as they saw them come running around the corner, Asmodeus headed up the ladder, tugging Ju Lan after him. Ellie was next up, followed by Dean, who slipped on the wet rungs as he fled for his life.

"Eren! The twins are dead!" Dean said as he reached the top of the ladder.

Eren went to close the hatch, but Dean stopped her. The twins' corpses climbed the ladder quickly and headed straight for Dean. Eren closed the hatch as Dean sprinted out of the office, chucking the LMG to Draxon as he and the twins ran up the stairs to the first floor and into an open room clear of personnel.

The two zombies cornered Dean and began to encroach on his position. He drew his baton again. As they charged him, he hit them to one side and ran past them, slamming the door and holding it shut.

Draxon and Eren joined him. Draxon took a small magnet from his back pocket and put it on the door frame, keeping the door locked.

Eren indicated the locked door. "Dean... what the hell?"

"I don't know what happened. We split up to close both entrances... there's a cave-in down there. It's only a little more secure... if at all" He sat against the wall, his eyes slightly brighter silver than before.

"Eren, can I talk to you for a second?" Draxon said. He and Eren moved out of Dean's earshot. He leant against the wall, listening to the groans from the room. The pain in his leg made him breathe through his teeth.

When Draxon and Eren returned, Dean was in tears, crying into his knees.

Draxon handed him a key card. "Dean. Go get some rest. Top floor, room eight."

Dean took it, bolting up the stairs with a limp. He ran past all the soldiers and quarantine crew and straight into the room Draxon had named, which was immaculate, with black walls and white furniture and bed sheets. Dean threw his gear to the floor and removed his boots, then sat on the bed, letting the tears flow.

A few hours later there was a knock on his door. He got up and opened it to see Ellie, who had red eyes from crying.

"Hey, Dean... can I come in?"

Dean let her in, and she sat on his bed in her gear.

He sat next to her. "You doing okay, Ellie?"

She shook her head. "I just watched them struggle with the door dude... I laughed... I didn't see the zombies coming until it was too late. I tapped on the radio, but the screams... I can't... I can't stop hearing them."

Dean unclipped and removed her plate carrier. "You should have a hot bath. According to the soldiers I passed on my way here, they have a large water tank set up on the roof. Plenty of water being sent to this building." He hung up her carrier, kicking his underneath the bed.

"Dude... I can't use your bath! What would everyone say?" She went to grab her plate carrier but Dean stopped her, holding her shoulders.

"I need you to wash here in my bathroom... otherwise, I can't... I won't risk getting caught with my pants down... literally or figuratively." Dean fell onto the floor, revealing a large gnash on his leg where his trousers were torn.

She stared at the fingernail scratches that cut deep into his flesh. "Dude, what happened?"

"I think Danni – or was it Danny? – I think one of them caught me as I tried to get past." He moved away from Ellie as she tried to get closer.

"Dean, you need to let me..."

Dean grabbed his pistol. "Ellie... I'm sorry, but could you go get Draxon for me?" He kept his pistol pointed at her until she left, then sighed with relief.

He looked down at his leg, sighed again, and then, responding to an instinct, he put his pistol in his mouth and pulled the trigger.

Everything was painful for a second before his vision went black. Dean felt as if he was floating in water, thick water. He smiled at the peacefulness of the new world he found himself in.

#

He opened his eyes to find that he wasn't dead. He was in a white room, and he couldn't move or see outside of the bathtub he lay in. He was covered in black sludge. The bathtub looked as if it could fit two adults, leaving Dean a lot of room. The room, too, was massive, and appeared expensive to build, with not a single crack in its white walls. The black sludge, or goo, was cold to the touch, but when Dean became too cold it heated up again. It was so thick that it restricted his movements.

Dean waited for someone to walk in. He hoped it would be Draxon or Eren – but it wasn't. It was Magnus Phoenix himself. He still wore his armour and coat, along with metal gauntlets with technology seamlessly woven into them, as suggested by the blinking gold light on Magnus's wrist. They were decorated with silver and gold, which seemed befitting for a royal.

"Sir..." Dean's eyes were still silver, and his wounds were practically all healed.

"Young man, are you aware of the consequences of your actions? My commander and my daughter both blame themselves. My granddaughter is worried and scared, and we have a devolved girl we've had to lock in a room. Our missions on the planet have been restricted due to numbers, and I've had to keep you in this healing tub for three days."

He came so close that Dean could smell his anger that, or Magnus had been drinking.

"Sir, I..." Dean couldn't come up with an excuse.

The tub began to drain and Dean found he could move once again.

"Now, Magnus said, "if I'm being honest, I want you expelled. But I've been forced to keep you on. So, as punishment, you are going back down to the planet and you are to do a tour outside of the tower. If you come back, you will be forgiven for your mistake. If you don't arrive back at the tower... well, you won't be our problem." He slapped a recording device, that looked a lot like a little black bar with a slider and a button, onto the side of the tub and walked out.

Dean got up and dressed in a uniform that had been laid out ready. Then he picked up the recorder and pressed play.

"Dean. I just want to commend you on your ability to put others first." It was Magnus's voice coming from the recording device. "You saw yourself as a threat and thought to remove that threat. As such, if you swing by the armoury I'll give you your kit for the planet."

Dean threw the device at the wall. "Threat? I'm always a threat!"

He stormed out of the room, forgetting his helmet and

pads, and strode straight to the pod room, where launched without any gear, crashing down towards the city.

When the pod had landed, he hopped out and clicked the 'return' button to send it home.

He looked towards the city centre; it was roughly twenty miles from where he had landed.

"If I don't die this time, I'll stop trying." Dean exhaled and began walking.

Just as it was starting to get dark, his radio activated. "Dean... why didn't you collect a weapon from the armoury?" Draxon's shaking voice filled Dean with fear.

"If it's not obvious, I want death to claim me!" he shouted into the radio. "I can't do this! I'm a threat to everyone I care about – I won't hurt them!"

A pod dropped on top of the tower.

"Dean, please... haven't we lost enough people to this planet? Will you let Travis's death, Archibold's death, Carrion's death all be in vain. Will you?" Draxon sounded defeated.

"I'm scared, and you did very little to reassure me... You even admitted to being afraid! How is that supposed to help? If you've survived for so long, had training as good or better than you gave us, how can you expect me to not want death to be quick? So why should I care? I don't even have a home to return to."

As Dean marched on, he heard footsteps all around him, scuttling in the trash, as well as distant screams that seemed to be getting closer.

"Dean, these creatures are worse at night... Without a weapon, you will die." Draxon no longer sounded afraid, only reassuring.

Dean stopped. "It's too late to change my mind now. If I die, all the problems will be fixed. This is for the best." He turned off his radio and dropped it into a drain. He marched on, only to tumble over some rubble, falling down and snapping his arm.

"*Fuck*," he breathed.

He rolled on his back in pain, stopping only when a group of zombies emerged from a damaged building. They gathered around, studying Dean as he lay there, panicking. Many of the zombies had been soldiers from the city, and a few were civilians, a couple of them children.

"Come on, then! Don't just stand there – kill me!" Dean yelled.

The zombies stumbled closer before retreating slightly.

"They cannot kill you."

The voice had come from the building. Moments later, a human boy no older than the girl Dean had saved came into view. He wore a blue hoodie and had a bag slung on his back. He spoke with a confidence beyond his age – not that Dean cared. Dean's arm was broken in two places and part of the bone had broken through the skin, the blood soaking into his uniform.

"What—" Dean forced himself to his feet, holding his broken arm with his other hand.

"They cannot kill you simply because you are already dead. Your eyes... they are soulless."

As the boy approached and the dead moved out of his way.

"Lucky me," Dean muttered. He began to walk, but the dead got in his way.

"When you return to your people, tell them to leave. The dead are amassing and you won't stave off a full attack." With that, the boy returned to the building, along with the zombies.

Dean stumbled on towards the large tower. Survivors crowded alongside him as he walked. The zombies stayed far away, gathering in the dark.

Dean remained silent. The survivors muttered around him, but he was too focused to listen. Some of them fell silent or even went missing on the journey.

Sometimes Dean saw white eyes in the dark, staring at both him and the survivors. He could hear the zombies talking, their voices strained and filled with pain and fear. They spoke not of death or fear, or of hunger or anger, but of peace and oneness. A joint mind, a joint consciousness, a joint pain.

The weather changed during the night, and it began to rain. The cold went all the way to Dean's boots. Still he kept walking, and so the survivors kept walking, those who stopped never catching up with the main group.

As Dean and around one hundred people arrived at the tower, the barricade parted, allowing Draxon to come running out. He brought Dean and the survivors inside, then closed the barricade. The survivors were taken to quarantine, whilst Dean was dragged inside the main building.

He sat Dean on a bench and signalled for a medic. "Dean. Saying that Magnus is pissed would be an understatement. As for me, you'll pay when you're feeling better."

Dean grabbed Draxon's plate carrier and pulled him in so no one else would hear. "Draxon, you need to get everyone out of here or call for more guns. The zombies... they're gathering for a strike."

"Alright, lad. You just rest... I'll deal with the zombies." With that, Draxon got up and left.

"Dean" said a middle-aged man with large brown horns and a white uniform with a red cross sewn onto the back.

"My name is Shrike. I'm going to knock you out for a couple hours and start to heal your arm. But I need to know something."

"What's that?" Dean looked at the large needle in Shrike's hand.

"What's your favourite colour?"

Before Dean could answer, Shrike had jabbed the needle into Dean's chest. Instantly, Dean fell unconscious.

#

When he finally burst into consciousness again, Dean's arm was fully healed, and he was alone.

He heard gunfire and shouting, and the screams of zombies as they charged at the barricade and the tower.

He rose to his feet to see the survivor girl, Dean had found whilst scaling the tower, running from a couple of survivors. He chased after them, heading for the roof.

When he finally caught up with them, they went to push her from the roof and into the horde below.

"Stop!" Dean shouted. Time itself seemed to listen, freezing everything from the birds to the people and even the atoms of dust falling all around them.

The girl and the men froze, and Dean wedged himself between them. Time resumed but the men were clearly confused. They ran away as another, much larger, wave of zombies approached the tower.

"They're here for me you know," the girl said, looking up at Dean, who was still watching the door. "You could come with me."

Dean looked over his shoulder at her. "Do you want to go with them?"

"Oh yes... At first I was scared, but now I'm perfectly fine. But no one will let me outside. It's not fair." She stamped her foot on the floor and crossed her arms stroppily.

"There's another way out, you know. I'll let you out if you can promise me everyone here will be allowed to leave."

As Dean knelt in front of her, she looked upwards and to the left, as if someone was standing there.

"I can promise that if you all start leaving now, you will make it... most of you. At least, that's what Papa says."

Dean put his hands over his face as if all the information he had been learning was far too much for him to handle. "Who is Papa?"

Once again, the girl looked to the left. "He says he

controls the zombies, but not fully, and that he can't stop them now. He can only distract them with me."

"Can you ask Papa exactly how much time we'd have? How many of my friends would make it?"

"He says everyone, if you leave now." She smiled, not knowing how little hope she was giving him.

"Let's go see Draxon. He may be able to help us." He held out his hand and she took it.

"Let's go, big brother. It's time for me to go outside and play." She skipped down the stairs beside him.

When they reached the bottom floor, Draxon was busy ordering cadets around. Most of them were fighting, but a few were helping with wounded troops and survivors.

Dean interrupted Draxon and Magnus talking over the radio as cadets left Draxon's side. "Draxon! We need to evacuate immediately – it's the only way to save everyone!"

"So you speak the truth," Magnus said. "He did arrive in one piece. Intriguing. Draxon, I believe the time has come for us to abandon this foolish attempt at rescue and save who we can. Evacuate immediately and bring the idiot back with you – my granddaughter is furious." He cut the radio off at his end.

Draxon smiled at Dean smiling, before punching the young teen hard in the stomach. "That was for shooting yourself in the head. Now what are you and her doing down here?" Draxon indicated the girl as he picked Dean up from the floor.

"She's our only chance to limit numbers so we can escape. Like I said, I spoke with a boy who—"

Draxon raised his hand, cutting Dean off. "That's exactly why I can't let her go. She's too valuable." He called over some guards, but as they approached another wave of zombies came sprinting over the corpses and breaking past the barricade.

"Let her use the tunnels to leave! We can all head to the roof and evacuate. As much as I hate it, we need to let go."

Dean said as he took the girl without a response from Draxon, and he moved the desk blocking the hatch in the security office.

"Follow this tunnel to the left as you climb down," he said. "When you reach a large metal door, turn left again and you'll see a cave-in."

He was about to let the girl start climbing when Draxon entered carrying a military backpack, which he put on her. "Some supplies for the road, kid," he said. "I assume since you're alive you still need food and water."

After the hatch was closed they left for the roof. Most of the horde had moved away from the tower, following the girl, but some broke through the riot gate and began heading up the tower. They caught a large group of survivors unprepared, though they slowed the stampede long enough for the rest to escape.

As they strapped into the pod, Dean noticed that Draxon appeared disturbed. He was thumbing something over in his hand, something small and metallic, he was looking directly at where the girl had left.

"You okay, Draxon?" Dean asked. "If you're still pissed, I'm sorry..."

Draxon shook his head. His bottom lip was quivering and his face was slightly red.

As the pod launched Dean could see the horde in full swing, running over buildings as if they were pebbles. Amid this sea of death was a small bit of pink, skipping happily safe and sound.

"I've killed children before, in the war," Draxon said. "Imperial schools and cities were prime targets for sabotage. I became very, very good at it. I even designed a charge small enough to fit in your backpack but that still packed a large punch. But it still never got any easier."

He held up a detonator and pulled the trigger, creating a devastatingly large explosion at the centre of the horde.

Dean looked on in shock as the horde burned. "Draxon... don't tell me it was the backpack."

"Orders, kid... I will always follow them to the letter." A tear ran down Draxon's scarred, deformed cheek, and he was biting on his quivering lip hard enough to draw blood.

"And if it was me that you were ordered to kill?" Dean asked, lurching forward in his restraints. "Or Ellie? Or Ju Lan?"

"I'd follow orders... because we are soldiers. Orders are what matter."

Dean sat back, repulsed. "You're wrong, Draxon. *People* are what matter – the people we fight for, and the people we fight against. I'd have thought you would have known that."

Draxon appeared about to speak, but no words came out. His expression of disappointment remained even after they had come in range of the academy.

#

"To lose sight of one's objective is common, but to reverse one's goal and one's fear is only achievable when a man is not truthful to himself."

– King Visceno V, *Kings and Queens Long Gone* by King Magnus Phoenix

Chapter Seven: Ranking and Demand

When the pod arrived at the academy, Magnus and a large group of medical personnel were waiting. Half the cadets had come back alive. One-eighth of the soldiers and doctors had returned, and thirty civilians from the colony had survived.

Dean pushed his way past Magnus and the medics to reach the elevator and pressed the button for the top floor. The elevator sputtered as it rose closer to Dean's sanctuary. He leant against the wall, eyes closed, just breathing. He thought back to the shuttle incident and Draxon's cold expression after he had killed the intruder. Then his mind took him even further back, to the lake where his brother had been attacked, and to his own face that reflected in the blood, as he killed the men he hated so much. He had looked directly at the face of a boy who enjoyed killing, the boy's eyes blacker than the night sky and a grin so wide his face looked like it might tear.

The elevator stopped and its doors opened. Ellie stood there, looking at Dean, who was motionless, half asleep.

"You're alive then, idiot?" Ellie said harshly as she stepped into the lift. It began to ascend once more.

Dean opened his eyes. "That's debatable."

"Dean. You have survived when others didn't... How?" Ellie put her hand on Dean's shoulder but he shrugged it off.

"It doesn't matter now, does it? I always survive when others don't. I'm always the one that's left standing. It doesn't matter if it's a fight or a race. It doesn't even matter if I want to win or not. I'm always the last one standing."

Dean stopped the elevator and got off at a random floor.

"Dean! Don't you turn your back on me!" Ellie yelled, getting the attention of many people as well as Dean.

"I'll turn my back on whoever I want to!" he retorted defensively. "If you have a problem with that, then go fetch your grandfather or Draxon! That way I can kill them with a clear conscience!" His eyes were almost black and his face was red with rage.

"What happened down there? Why are you being so rude?"

As Ellie closed in, Dean looked to his left to see Magnus and Draxon coming up a flight of stairs. It was clear they'd been running, and Draxon still hadn't removed his weapons.

"Ask them." Dean pointed to Magnus and Draxon before marching away, his arms swinging angrily at his sides.

Eventually, he reached a balcony overlooking the asteroid city of Phoenix Academy. He sighed and murmured to himself, "What did you do, Dean?"

He turned to see Magnus standing behind him.

"Cadet, I assume something is bothering you, beyond the death of the young girl" Magnus too looked out over his Academy. Dean noticed his hair was slightly out of place, Magnus the king whose entire existence was supposed to be perfect was flawed.

"The boy… he said I'm soulless. I watched many people die, and I've killed my share… but you're wrong… I don't feel anything for the young girl. That's why I'm freaked out." Dean tightened his grip on the railing.

Magnus leant forward to get a better look at Dean's face. "Come with me," he said, and began walk away, but Dean didn't follow him.

Magnus stopped in the doorway and half-turned to look at Dean out of the corner of his eye. The king's golden retinas produced a burning sensation on the back of Dean's neck.

"That wasn't a suggestion, it was an order." Magnus waited for Dean, who looked out at the Academy for a few more seconds before standing up straight and joining him.

They walked hurriedly down many stairs, eventually arriving at a laboratory at the very bottom of the station. The area appeared old, some of the walls covered in rust and even the doors an orangey brown. The lights flickered on and off gently, one red and one yellowy white. The door had the Verantian letters for L and B but the rest of the word was covered with layers of rust and grime.

"What is this place?" Dean asked. As the lights blinked on, he examined the extremely old equipment within the room filled with dust and cobwebs. The windows seemed iced over and the floor was covered in clutter.

"My oldest lab, from when I was just a scientist in an old vault." Magnus began to power up a machine, which began to whir. The rusted table upon which it stood began to vibrate gently. A piece of old wood was the only thing keeping one of the table legs up.

"What does that do?" Dean asked as he approached it.

Magnus tapped the dusty wooden stool in front of the machine. "It's old technology. But research into other items like it stopped when the Imperium took over – a choice I regret now. But it should still work." Magnus stood behind the machine, typing into the large keyboard at the rear of the machine.

"But what does it do?" Dean looked around the device. On the outside was an amalgamation of wires and metal with one glass screen and what looked like eyeholes.

"This is going to tell me exactly what your evolution is and what you can do." Magnus grinned as he came back around the machine and forced Dean to look into it. A yellow light scanned up and down Dean's eyes constantly.

Dean sat for three hours as Magnus poured over the screens, searching for something. Dean let his eyes relax, and the machine stopped a few minutes later.

"I have two lots of good news and some bad news," Magnus said as he shut down the machine. He led Dean out of the lab, then struggled to close the doors and locked them.

"What's the bad news?" Dean asked.

Magnus handed him a badge. "You just got promoted. The good news is that you have, in fact, evolved to something stronger than a royal. You've become a warrior class Verantian. The even better news is that you have a soul... You just need to get better acquainted with your new self. Now head off to bed – trial results come in tomorrow and tutors will be assigned to squads."

#

When Dean entered his room, he found Ju Lan curled up on his bed like a dog and Ellie sitting in a chair, waiting for him. She watched him from the moment he entered.

"Do you need her to move?" she asked, indicating Ju Lan.

Dean shook his head. "No. I sleep on the floor. What're

you doing here?" He glanced at the folded-out bed next to the window.

"I'm here to make sure you don't do something stupid, I'm under orders from the top." Ellie pointed to the ceiling.

Dean sat in his corner. Ellie had a light directly behind her head, which gave Dean the impression that she was wearing a halo.

"I'm not going to..." Dean looked at the sleeping Ju Lan, his silver eyes full of questions. His voice filled with regret as he said, "Hey, Ellie?"

"Yes?" Ellie approached and sat on the bed.

"I'm sorry. I, uh... I'm just sorry."

Ellie noticed the badge in his hand. "You don't need to be sorry, dude. You just need to confide in me if you're not feeling too good. It's what friends are for. So what rank did he give you?" She smiled and held out her hand.

Dean handed over the thick metal badge. Ellie looked it over, seeming unsure. Her face told Dean everything, from the fact she already knew he was getting promoted and from the fact that he had no intention of trying anything again, but she kept smiling. The metal badge was brand new and shone like a well-polished boot. It was shaped like a shield and had the Verantian letters for CPT written across it.

"I'm sure whatever rank this is, you earned it." Ellie clipped it to Dean's shirt and went to get up, but Dean grabbed her arm. He continued looking at the floor as he said, "I've got an... odd request. Can you... sit on my lap? Until I fall asleep. My brother normally would, but he's not here." Dean's cheeks went red, and he tried not to look Ellie in the eyes.

"Um... Yeah, sure... but only till you fall asleep." Slowly, Ellie lowered herself until she and Dean were firmly in the corner between the set of drawers and the wall.

Dean played with Ellie's hair for a while, but soon fell asleep. His night was peaceful and he dreamed he was back home, having dinner with his family.

When he awoke, Ellie was still on his lap, sound asleep. Ju Lan was sitting cross-legged on the bed, staring at them both. Her hair was messy and curly, and her eyes appeared normal.

Ellie's buttocks were on Dean's left leg, and her body and head leant against his left side. She was breathing gently into his neck and chest. He smiled, forgetting Ju Lan staring at them.

"You two are so cute together," she said. "You should

think about asking her out."

Dean tried to think how to respond. The smell coming from Ju Lan was offensive, but until now he hadn't realised just how bad it was. In contrast, Ellie smelled like home.

"You're back?" Dean said, keeping his voice low to avoid waking Ellie. "How do you feel?"

Ju Lan stretched. It was clear her body was more developed from the devolution detox, and her hair was long and curly, not to mention very, very messy. She wore her glasses, which made her red eyes glint.

"Odd," she said. "But that's parasites for you. I see your parasite evolved you. Lucky. Devolution is reversible with time and mental exercises, but not evolution – no you're stuck silver-eyed forever." Ju Lan smiled, then picked up a pillow from the bed and threw it at Ellie, waking her up.

"Oh my god! Dean, I'm sorry! I must have fallen asleep!" Ellie shot to her feet, then looked at Ju Lan.

"I'm back," Ju Lan said. She and Ellie hugged excitedly, almost dancing on the spot, but Ellie was watching as Dean grabbed spare clothes from the drawers.

"I'm going to get dressed in the bathroom," he said. "If I were you two, I'd change too. Especially you, Ju... I don't think they got you to bathe." Dean walked past them.

His unintentional insult cut deep. After he closed the door, he heard angry footsteps, then silence and then laughter.

He got changed, throwing his dirty laundry into a chute, having taken the badge off his shirt beforehand.

As he left the bathroom he noticed some clothes on the floor. He went red, backtracking into the bathroom from which he could hear Ellie and Ju Lan laughing loudly.

He waited until someone knocked on the door before leaving and smiling in embarrassment at the girls.

"Next time, use the bathroom," Dean said, straightening his shirt.

As they headed out, the girls laughed behind him as they walked.

"Dean, are you not comfortable with naked girls?" Ellie asked as they got into the elevator at the other side of the floor below their rooms.

"No. I was taught to respect privacy and your right to expose yourselves to the man, or men, you love," Dean said, going very red.

He looked around the elevator, which was clean and appeared relatively new. However it was so small that Dean had no choice but to touch shoulders with the girls.

"Quaint – but we aren't human. Verantian culture has always allowed for openness between sexes," Ellie said, stretching gently and smiling as her hand grazed Dean's neck gently.

"Please, princess," Ju Lan said, poking Ellie's skinny ribs, "both me and Dean come from humble backgrounds, and I'm not even sure who my real dad is. My mum was pregnant with me when the man who raised me married her."

"Look, it's not that," Dean said. "I just don't know what I'm doing when it comes to girls. I don't know what to say or do, so I get embarrassed. Until a girl proves to me I'm doing the right thing, I'm afraid that won't change."

He stopped the elevator at the appropriate floor and hopped off. The girls walked slightly behind him, muttering, whilst trying not to let other students hear what they were saying.

Dean checked his new badge that weighed his uniform down. No one else had one. When they arrived at the large auditorium, he saw that every seat had a number. Dean and Ellie were front row, with Ju Lan having been given a spot on the floor, which made Ellie giggle.

It wasn't long before Eren noticed that Ju Lan was no longer devolved. She fetched her a chair and gave her a quick check over.

The hall filled slowly until all but one seat, in the centre of the front row, was occupied. Draxon was nowhere to be seen.

The hall was enormous. It had several hundred seats and the lights made it heat up incredibly fast. The room had been redecorated recently with brand new flooring and new paint on the walls. Dean could still see a little of the old blue paint behind the stage.

Magnus walked onto the stage and looked around, not smiling.

"A warm welcome to the students of the year 2202. I would like to inform you of some developments, as well as announce your ranks, departments, and teams of four. However, before we start, I would like to take the time to address a few students who don't like obeying restricted signs. Now, I'm sure, considering what you all who decided not to obey saw in that last room, that you understand this is not a place of pure safety, and that by breaking the rules you nearly caused catastrophe for all." Magnus and the everybody in the hall looked to the side doors as they opened. Draxon entered in full gear, with blood on his boots.

"As for ranks," Magnus continued, "those of you in the front row all performed admirably, and achieved high scores in your trial tests, so you all get relatively high ranks – the highest being Dean Ivanova, with Cadet Captain." Uproar from the students near the back filled the room until all the students were shouting.

As Magnus waited for it to finish, Dean was shrinking in his chair. Obviously a report had gone around about his escapade and the fact that the two humans he had been given command of were dead – and that they had not died quickly.

On the other side of Draxon, Asmodeus rose using his tail to make himself visible to all. He started clapping until everyone was ca;;ping and the sound filled the hall. Then he and everyone else stopped, allowing Magnus to continue.

"Thank you, Asmodeus. As for your own rank, you rank third, a Cadet Sergeant." Magnus threw Asmodeus a badge and Dean stood up, applauding him along with the others. "Ellie Phoenix, you rank second, with Cadet First Lieutenant." He threw a badge to Ellie, who caught it.

Dean applauded for her, along with only a few others. To the back of the classroom, some old Earthen slurs were yelled out, and some people laughed. Draxon held the back of Dean's collar so he didn't jump up to attack them.

"As for Ju Lan, Edward Canary, Silicia Song and Chris Whatford-James, you four achieved the rank of Cadet

Corporal. Well done, you four." After another short round of applause, Magnus walked to the centre of the stage and looked directly at Draxon, smiling.

"A bit of a rare occasion," he continued, "but Commander Black has recently returned from his four hundredth mission, and for this I award him the rare honour of Commander General, giving him command of not only this facility's troops, but also all Varantian forces and the human forces that assist us." Magnus clapped loudly, followed by Ellie and the others – everyone apart from Dean.

Draxon remained seated, but he leant forward to look at Dean, who sat silent with clenched fists. As Draxon leant back, a look of disappointment crossed his face. Eren watched heartbroken from the side of the room.

"Right… the second and third rows all achieved Cadet Lance-Corporal. Your badges are under your seats. To everyone else, I can only say that in order to achieve a rank, you must work hard and you must shine. Which means volunteering." Magnus gazed at the annoyed but hopeful crowd. "Now, to the subject of lessons. You all must attend Maths, English, Verantian and History. Some of you will be forced to take simple tactics, some will be forced into more advanced classes. Range days are every Saturday, whilst Sunday, the day of rest becomes the day you all work your butts off in your own time to achieve your goals and pass the tests. Congratulations, all of you, and I look forward to seeing what comes next." Magnus led one more wave of applause before dismissing everyone.

He hadn't spoken about most of the subjects he had said he could cover, and students were laughing about it as they left.

As the students left, Draxon grabbed by the arm Dean to hold him back. Dean stood facing away from Draxon, Ellie and Ju Lan, who were waiting at the door, watching him. Dean seemed like he was ready to let loose a howl of a scream, his fists clenched tightly.

"Dean, I really am sorry about what happened… but even if you can't forgive me, you still need to show me respect as your teacher."

Draxon was caught off guard as Dean spun on the heel of his boot. "*Respect* you? I do respect you. It's the only reason I haven't hit you, and it's the only reason I let you keep me behind. But I will *not* celebrate the death of an innocent young girl. That I will never do." He spun again, marching away, his footsteps echoing in Draxon's ears.

Dean, Ellie, and Ju Lan headed back to their room with only the thundering of Dean's boots breaking the silence.

Once they arrived, Dean went straight to the corner, where he punched the wall, cracking it.

"Dean... what happened?" Ellie asked as she approached Dean, who was now leaning against the wall.

"You know the little girl... from the fifth city... The one that... that called me big brother..." Dean leant on his arm.

Ellie sat on the bed beside Ju Lan. "Yeah, of course I do. Magnus told me she didn't make it."

"Didn't make it? He ordered Draxon to strap a bomb to her back and kill her... and Draxon just *did* it." Dean stopped leaning on his arm and instead just sat against the wall.

"Dean... I'm so sorry..." Ellie moved down to rest his head on her shoulder.

Ju Lan moved down to the floor and sat on the other side of Dean. She wiggled around for a bit before smiling and looking around.

"What's up, Ju?" Dean asked.

Ju Lan smiled wider. "The floor is ridiculously more comfortable than those beds." She got up, folded up the sheets and put the pillows on the floor. "Come on – let's prank Draxon and Magnus."

Dean, Ellie, and Ju Lan moved the overly large mattress out into the hall and bent it till it fit in the elevator, then closed the doors. Before they had realised what they had done, the elevator began to slowly grind its way down to the lower floors.

Ju Lan then took the portable bed apart and used its ribbing to build a sled, which she loaded with pillows and sheets from Ellie's room as well as her clothes and Ellie's clothes.

Then she took them all into Dean's room, and they filled the drawers with tightly folded and rolled clothes and Dean's corner with polished and dirty boots.

When Draxon entered to ask about the mattress, he found all three of them tightly wrapped in makeshift sleeping bags, all asleep inside the shell of what had been the double bed. Both girls had an arm resting on Dean's chest and Dean looked as happy as could be imagined.

Draxon laughed silently and snapped a picture on his tablet. He sent it to Eren and Magnus and awaited their responses.

Aww, how cute! I'm totally taking the piss out of this, Eren wrote, her handwriting appearing on the background of Draxon's tablet.

If he does anything, I swear to the kings... Magnus began, but Draxon stopped reading and left the room.

As part of his rounds, he made his way round all the students' rooms, using the scanners to detect how many bodies were inside.

When he came upon a student's bedroom with a *Restricted Area* sign on the door, he used the scanner to see into the room. It detected four heat sources, two of them very small, inside one of the others.

"Holy flames... they mated!" Draxon said in shock.

Report on Subject Two

To the heads of the science union and the King.

Based on the findings by our boots on the ground during both incursions, we have discovered that the parasite involved in the changing of chemicals in the brain was always ingested through water.

However, it is also surmised that, given time, this parasite can and will evolve. We still don't know if the parasite is native to the planet or if it's been delivered by an outside source, but I can determine that since the second incursion into Colony Habitat Five, also referred to as the fifth colony, the parasite has evolved once more.

This time, the parasite has not only evolved in the sense of who it can take over, but also in the sense of reproduction.

Subject One is a male human teen and Subject Two is a female human teen. These circumstances, as well as them being locked in a room with no food, has allowed for them to be proactive in certain ways, leading to a double pregnancy in the female subject.

We will be monitoring the progress daily, but upon return to the fifth colony, if required, we will have a separate team from the main group deliver them into the horde to observe what happens.

On a separate note, we introduced several chemicals to our older subjects and found that chlorine kills the parasites and, if undamaged, the brain returns to its previous persona.

Luckily, several of our better grunts were rescued, although as humans always seem to die immediately, I can surmise this is due to the chemical structure of the protective gel around the brain. A Verantian brain is made for a warrior and thus less likely to break due to poisonous weapons of most kinds, as well as reducing pain – whereas humans are not so fortunate.

Our Commander General has found that there is an intelligence to these creatures. From my own experience, this is hard to understand, but from the new results and the fact that the parasite and children to be born are not separate but combined... it seems we could be looking at a brand-new type of life form.

I theorise that – if they survive – these children may, in fact, have full control of the indicated hive mind that has previously been detected, shared between subjects. In addition, a third expedition to the first site came back negative for the hive mind that once existed there. If it is stealthy enough to cross into the fifth colony, then the other colonies may already be infested and beyond saving.

I will attach the following graphs, which indicate certain factors that we checked when both events started.

Hopefully one of the great minds reading this report will notice a similarity to indicate a trigger moment.

– graph showing random weather over three weeks

– graph showing population increases

– carbon footprint graph

– power usage graph

– military presence graph

– list of ships that docked at the third colony.

Please note any findings and add to the report at a later date.

Signed,

Eren Phoenix

Chapter Eight: Attack of the Lessons

Dean awoke later that day with the girls on either side of him. His tablets alarm was going off, as was Ellie's. He lay in the middle of the girls, blushing like a traffic light and unable to move.

In their sleep their makeshift sleeping bags had come apart and the girls had made their way closer to Dean until they were nearly swallowing him, the both of them wrapping their arms around him, faces almost touching.

Ellie rolled over once more, practically burying Dean under both girls. Ellie opened her eyes, her face level with Dean's and her eyes staring into his.

"Ellie... morning." Dean said with a smile, his face as red as a tomato.

"Morning. What's that sound?" Ellie pushed herself up. She hadn't put on pyjamas and her shirt was undone, revealing a black vest underneath.

"It's the tablet – it's been sounding off for a while." Dean rolled from the bed, stood up and walked to the tablet.

When he had rolled over, he had pushed Ellie to the floor, and her shirt had shifted slightly to the left, revealing a burn mark on her shoulder. Dean didn't stare at it, instead looking her in the eyes.

"Ellie, get Ju up. We have history in eight minutes."

Dean put on his boots as Ellie woke Ju Lan up. They each grabbed their tablets and sprinted from the room, down the stairs and to an old room that had a sign outside "Cartography" far from the bedrooms. Ellie didn't button up her shirt until they arrived at its door.

They had run so far that they had seen more of the Academy than they had in the first week. Most of the Academy was so advanced that it seemed like a pinnacle of advancement and of education. There were parts, however, that seemed like they were salvaged from an old mining station or some other place even more exposed to the harshness of existence.

The room was already full. Draxon stood at the front of the room wearing full military gear. The other students were writing something on their tablets and Draxon was scratching inside his boot.

He looked up at the three students as they entered and pointed to a desk right at the front.

"You three are almost late. Tell me, was it due to the lack of a mattress, or was your company just too pleasant for each other?"

Ellie tried to speak but nothing came out.

"We just need to set an alarm for earlier, that's all," Dean said, his tone calm but spiteful, like when you have a disdain for someone but you can't openly voice it.

He sat down between the girls once more.

"Wait," Ellie protested, suddenly finding her voice. "What gives you the right to just walk into Dean's room like that?"

"Maybe, cadet, the fact that this Academy, like all others, is first and foremost a military institution. That means we use the rules of the Verantian army and navy," Draxon replied in annoyance.

"We were nearly late – whatever," Ju Lan said. She seemed half asleep still. "Can we start, please?"

Draxon made a disappointed scowl at the three of them before starting his lesson. "Today we will be learning about the first and last battle between the Verantia Prime defences and the Imperial Navy. As someone who fought in this battle, I can say that this engagement made us stand out enough to not be purged, unlike a few of our allies." Draxon clicked his fingers and small holograms appeared on everyone's desks.

"Sir… how did the Verantians stand out?" one of the human students at the back of the room asked. "The war with the Imperial Navy couldn't have been that different."

"We fought an armada of laser-gun-wielding maniacs whose obsession with power clouded their judgement." Draxon coughed after he had finished speaking.

"What were the Verantians fighting with?" another

human student asked.

"The Verantian forces were equipped with many different weapons, the most advanced being a giant cannon using gunpowder to project an explosive shell that could pierce any armour the Imperials brought. However, we had good reason for our lack of technology." Draxon clicked his fingers again and the hologram showed the planet Verantia and its three moons.

Ellie smiled as she spun the hologram with a flick of her hand. "Oh yeah, my grandfather talks of this often. Our moons were full of minerals that disrupt ion engines and screw with laser technology. When the Imperial Navy arrived they couldn't maintain orbit, so they had to leave sending drop pods instead."

"True. This ultimately cost them every battle, and our moons also stopped their powers from working, giving us the biggest advantage we could hope for." Draxon clicked his fingers again and the moons exploded, debris raining down on the planet.

"They destroyed the moons?" a human class member asked sadly.

"They did. The debris caused issues that we had long seen coming, which led to our planet becoming almost uninhabitable." Draxon stepped out from behind his desk.

"The siege lasted a week and the empire destroyed all three of our moons in just over an hour. The war lasted twenty years. The massacre afterwards lasted fifteen months and the peace talks lasted eight minutes. What you all need to do is to write down any thoughts you have – if you need more information on this topic, check the history tab on your tablets. Oh, and please use the dates and numbers provided... I didn't write five books for nothing. You have an hour. Begin." Draxon clapped and the holograms vanished.

Ju Lan looked up. "You wrote these books, sir?"

Draxon nodded. "History is the one subject where you can look to the future by studying the mistakes of the past. The first person to tell me the mistakes made by the Verantians gets to walk out of this class and go somewhere else." Draxon sat down at his desk and started to take off his gear.

"Waiting," Dean said loudly.

Everyone looked at him.

"What was that Dean?" Draxon asked as he took off his plate carrier.

"The Verantian forces garrisoned the homeworld and waited for the Imperials. We had our own ships with weapons that could easily combat the fleet at the entrance to our nebula. But we waited until they came over and blew us up – we were passive, and it cost us our moons and our world." Dean closed his tablet and stood up.

"You certainly have some strong feelings about this." Draxon rose to remove his belt, then sat down again.

"When you look at the bigger picture, your mistakes that day cost my brother his legs and us our freedom... You fucked it up for us. That was the mistake you made."

Knowing that Draxon understood he wasn't only talking about the Perpetual War, Dean left. He walked the almost empty halls only to run right into a teacher he had only ever seen once, who was wearing an engineering jumpsuit and a welding mask and caked in oil and grime. He walked with a slight limp and his left hand was missing his ring finger. He was carrying some rolled up paper plans under his arm.

"Cadet Captain Ivanova... aren't you supposed to be in history class at this very moment?"

"I am, but the Commander let me out early. I'm off to my next class – advanced tactics, in the large auditorium."

Dean made to move onwards, but the teacher grabbed his arm. "I can't let you wait there for an hour. Here, you can help me with some things – your hands seem small enough." The teacher beckoned and Dean followed.

They, Dean and Mr Venderfro headed to one of the lowest floors and entered a large hangar with hundreds of mechanics and cadets running around. It seemed just as hectic as the day Dean and the others had landed, but the shuttle was gone and so were most of the missiles.

"You have cadets here already. Why not get them to help you?" Dean said, putting his tablet on a workbench.

Mr Venderfro led him to a large engine. The rest of the vehicle it belonged to was covered with sheets. "Because they are idiots. Now reach and tell me what you feel." He walked Dean around to the front.

Dean rolled up his sleeve, then reached inside the engine as far as he could. "There's a jagged hole, elbow length in, and what feels like an expanded shell casing positioned sideways. Did this get shot at?" He pulled out a small object. When he washed the grime off, he realised it was a Syndicate charged round that had found its way inside the engine.

"Yes. This Verantian WarHawk arrived just after you left the station the first time. It was shot at and returned fire. Luckily it came home – the Syndicate attacker won't." The teacher signalled to an engineer and whispered to him.

"Sir, can I go back to my room and wash up?" Dean asked.

The teacher shook his head. "No. I still need a hand. Whilst the engineers deal with this, I need you to test my new device." He beckoned and Dean followed him once more.

They exited the hangar and entered a large lab to one side of it. The interior was full of weapons for ground and space combat. On the table was a new sleek rifle using the same .308 ammo as the rifle Dean used on the Colony.

Instinctively, Dean picked it up. It was very light and had an inbuilt sight, its settings adjustable with a small knob. It also had an inbuilt torch and laser sight, and a hidden, strong bipod attachment that Dean wouldn't have seen had he not caressed the rifle during his initial inspection.

"Like it, Captain?" the teacher asked.

Dean nodded. "I do. It's a good weight, a good size. The sight is decent and it requires no extras – well, maybe a suppressor." Dean put the rifle back on the table.

"I've built it to replace our standard rifle, but it's very hard to clean in the field. Not that it'll get that dirty – it's a good design. But what I actually need you to test is this." The teacher handed Dean a Verantian sword, which had a subtle curve and was sharp on both edges.

"It's a sword," Dean said as he swung it around clumsily with very little enthusiasm.

"It's made from a new metal. Supposed to be indestructible. Same as the rifle." The teacher picked up a large wrench and swung it at Dean, who blocked it with the sword, cutting the wrench in two.

"That makes sense." Dean placed the sword down before

the teacher could attack him again.

"You may leave for your room now, Captain. May I advise you to take the rifle to the armoury, along with the blade. Log them under your name."

The teacher gave Dean both items, then kicked him out of the lab.

Dean walked to the armoury, where he had a guard lock the gear up for him, before heading to his room. He thought back to the teacher, who had never removed the blast shield from his face. For some reason Dean had felt nervous around him – more nervous than when he had a gun pointed at him. Something wasn't right.

His tablet buzzed, breaking his concentration. It was from the same teacher.

Dean, please keep coming to help me. It would look good on your record and may result in a promotion or two. Plus, I can help you get ahead in some engineering aspects. It's always good to know all aspects of a mission, even the mechanical machinations of war.

The teacher had sent Dean a direct request and he seemed fine with that so he shrugged off his previous thoughts and responded, *Of course. I will come for twenty minutes or so after every lesson and spend my lunch and break times assisting you. I want to learn as much as I can and progress within the ranks.*

Feeling that this was a perfectly adequate response, Dean went about his day without giving it a second thought.

#

Over the next few months, Dean showed up to every single lesson without fail and even when people were blatantly speaking about him, he ignored them. Even when they were saying he awas a syndicate spy or the time someone spread the rumour he had laid with Ellie and Ju Lan.

He, Ellie, and Ju Lan would all turn up to lessons at the same time, but after each one Dean would visit the engineering teacher and Ellie and Ju Lan would 'lose contact' with him for several hours in a day combined between and after classes finished.

On the fourth morning of the galactic calendar month Veshitaros, Dean, Ellie and Ju Lan were in history class with Draxon, learning about the old priests of Verantia Prime.

"The first priest of our people was his high honour Ytresidortiso, pronounced Tres-i-dort-so," Draxon stated. "He was the one who first communed with our gods and brought the glint of the sacred flame back from the other side." He showed a very old, grizzled man wearing poorly maintained furs.

A human girl raised her arm high in the air to ask a

question. “Sir, what do you mean by the glint of the sacred flame?”

“The sacred flame is the name of our god’s place of residence. Whilst most deem it to be only a myth, half a dozen priests have said that they have visited, or even seen in its entirety, the sacred flame.”

Draxon switched the image to show another priest, this time a young girl around Dean’s age. “This is Tristania Forus Toruns Terani. She was the first priest to lead our people’s religion into space. She set up several Serenity-class stations for worship and light-bringing throughout the nebula that contains our homeworld. However, since her death, the locations of the fifteen stations in the orbit of our nebula-covered sun have been lost to the ages.” He showed an image of a space station designed to look like a flaming torch.

“Wait – not even one?” a human boy said from the very back of the room.

Draxon laughed. “No, not even one. However, we are not in a rush to find them. And if I’m frank, I would’ve thought that you guys would have an issue having our original homeworld encased in a nebula and having a sun at the same time, truth is we aren’t sure why there is a nebula but the smartest minds have come to the conclusion that it was artificial and bleeds energy from our sun to stop it from creating a supernova or worse, a black hole."

"Why not look for them? Surely recovering our past, even now... surely that would be a good idea?" Ellie said, attracting Draxon's attention.

"To recover them would mean entering our nebula again. Only a select few know the entrances that avoid using the opening that is under control by the Imperials. They did, after all, build the satellite that ripped the hole in the nebula wall. Also, discovering the satellites that lead to the sun would only be accomplishable when there is peace in the galaxy, as a Forx and an Imperial are necessary to open the supposed gate. This is not likely for at least a few years yet."

Dean put his hand up. "Draxon. What's a Forx?"

Draxon coughed and brought up the picture of a fox-like woman. "This is a Forx, an intelligent race that appear like humanoid foxes. Largely considered the most beautiful of races, and one of only two animalistic races not to confederate for peace four thousand years ago." He changed the hologram, ignoring the hands that shot up in response to his statement.

The lesson ended in silence. When everyone was getting up to leave, both of the girls looked at Dean.

"We have some questions for Draxon," Ellie said with a smile. "You go on ahead."

Dean simply nodded and left.

"You have questions for me?" Draxon asked as Ju Lan followed Dean to the door to watch him walk down the corridor.

"No," Ellie replied, "but we want to follow Dean, and we can't do that if we walk with him, because he always seems to get away from us."

Draxon sighed. "Come here, then." He guided them to his computer and entered his password into it.

"Eren? Really? You're the head of all our ground forces and the tactical advisor to the king... yet your password is the name of the woman you love?" Ellie said, looking bitterly disappointed.

"Easy to remember," Draxon replied, laughing.

They watched Dean stalk the halls. When he arrived at the lab, Draxon zoomed in on the engineering teacher.

"Hmm." Draxon zoomed in on the lab just before the doors closed. Then something made him race for the door.

"Draxon, what's up? Hey!" Ellie charged after him and Ju Lan followed, leaving Draxon's computer unlocked for everyone to see.

As Ellie and Draxon, trailed by an exhausted Ju Lan, ran through the corridors, they grabbed as many soldiers as they could, Draxon snatching the pistol of one who was laughing with his comrades obnoxiously as he ran past.

Draxon and Ellie stopped at the door to the hangar.

"Take Ju Lan to Dean's room, now," Draxon commanded.

Ellie, being Ellie, crossed her arms defiantly. "He's my friend! Draxon, what is going on? You seem more scared than on the planet!" she shouted, attracting attention from the hangar. The lab doors shut tight, and a red light signalled lockdown protocols.

"Isolated incidents, my arse!" Draxon yelled, banging his hand on the door frame. "Incinerated by accident, my arse! It's the fucking *Syndicate*, so do as you are told!"

The door frame crumpled into the wall. Ellie rushed away, terrified, grabbing Ju Lan as she ran.

Draxon looked at the pistol in his hand, then ran to the lab and began to unlock the door.

#

Meanwhile...

Dean was inside the lab, testing a new SMG design. He was making a few adjustments and had placed the weapon down to pick up a tool, as he had done hundreds of times before, when before he knew what was happening a metal pipe made contact with the side of his head.

He came around, groggy and concussed, to see blood on the table alongside the petri dishes, test tubes and glass flasks. Next to them was a tray of metal tools covered in blood – blood he knew was his own.

He was scared and cold, and his blood was running down his legs. Something else was wrong. He was hurting, but it wasn't the same sensation as cuts or scars.

"You know, when I heard the King was setting up this Academy, I was thrilled," his teacher's voice said. It was unconfined by the normal welding mask and clear as if he was right by Dean's ear. "A chance to experiment on Verantian children... perfect. Now I have a Verantian Warrior to experiment on... This will be sweet."

"Let me go... please, let me go." Dean looked around, but the teacher put a bag over Dean's head and tightened restraints, which seemed to be simple cable ties, fixing his wrist to the locked drawers of the desk. Dean's feet were tied with rope to the legs of the desk, making blood rush to his ankles.

"Oh no, not just yet. First, how about a history lesson, hmm? Do you know that there were once hundreds of colonies for both of our peoples in these skies? Did you? It's okay if you didn't. The Perpetual War obliterated them all, from Verantia Prime all the way to Estonia IV, thirty-five galaxies away. Thirty-five galaxies – that sure is a hell of a lot of planets. Oh well." This was the moment Dean knew this was no teacher but an agent of the syndicate.

The agent put something metallic onto Dean's exposed buttock and cut deep, making Dean scream in pain and in terror.

After only a few seconds, the sound of a glass container being pushed along the metal table made Dean look left and then right. More blood trickled down his leg.

"Sorry, Dean, I know it hurts. But in my defence, you didn't exactly make it easy for me. No, you're just like your father. The one man I couldn't get to. Oh, I tried, but your mother got in the way. She died, as you know, but she certainly beat me. Gave me my scars. Strong woman. Your dad too – he was strong, he led his fleet to thousands of planets, hundreds of systems and in every single one he defeated the odds, defeated the best of the best – and for what? The future? No, your father and the King are smart men. *Were* smart men. They did what thousands of people in history have tried to do: they played the game to win."

"Only your father played the game for Magnus, and Magnus played for... something. That's the mystery. I'm sure I'll figure it out eventually. But I digress – back to your father. He was the man who crippled the Imperium and the Syndicate. He destroyed every single school, university, library, and data storage centre, and he did it in the span of two days. A miracle worker. He set us back hundreds of years in all sectors, from economics to medication and even, to a degree, space flight. Your dad did it all, and with only a single fleet. Remarkable."

The agent stuck a needle into Dean's arm and drew blood, and maybe some bone marrow, Dean wasn't sure but he definitely felt all his bones and every inch of skin.

"Please, just stop..." Dean pleaded. "I'm sorry about all that. Please."

"Oh don't be sorry. Him doing all that allows me this pleasure, this honour! You see, I get to torture you and your people legally and happily, in the name of science. Now then, where next, Dean? I'll let you choose." The agent put some things on the table, Dean couldn't tell but they sounded like a mix of metal instruments a doctor or surgeon might use, although he definitely heard a ball peen hammer.

Dean didn't have a chance to answer.

A voice said, "I think not."

Draxon's voice was like an angel to Dean's tortured soul, a bell splitting the silence of hell.

The next sound was a loud gunshot and then Dean heard a body drop. Finally, he heard the pressurised sound of the doors opening, and the air became considerably colder.

Dean cried under the hood, then listened. He heard footsteps: loud, angry, quick. He heard voices but his concussion was kicking in. Even within the bag, he could tell his vision was blurred. He struggled against his restraints, crying. He could feel the cold of the table and the chill in the air, both of which scared him, he didn't know why but he was terrified.

"Dean, I'm going to take the bag off your head," Draxon said. "Then I'm going to guide you to your room and afterwards we are going to talk – not immediately, but eventually. You are going to feel bad – terrible and worthless. You're going to feel like less than nothing. All you need to know is that this sort of violation doesn't wash off, and we are here for you."

Dean couldn't find any words. He just put back on his uniform and left with Draxon, looking around at all the mechanics and cadets, who were simply staring at him. Security ran into the laboratory, sidearms drawn.

On the journey to his room, the crowded corridors were filled with his story, muttered like a Chinese whisper. As they approached his room, Dean stopped.

"Dean..." Draxon kept Dean hidden from the students who were watching like vultures from the stairs, trying to get a look at Dean. They wanted to see the mighty captain who cared for no one, brought down from his high horse.

"Can you get them out... just for a few nights?" Dean asked.

He stood aside, and Draxon went into his room without another word. Soon, Ellie and Ju Lan emerged and went into Ellie's old room.

"If you need anything," Draxon said, "just tap the door twice. One of my men will be here the whole time."

He was about to leave, but Dean put his arm out to stop him. "You'll get that written work you set. And the other teachers too. I still want the same work as everyone else." With that, Dean walked into his room and closed the door.

Ellie had been watching Dean from the door to her room. She hadn't yet been told why she wasn't allowed to see him in the lab, or just what was going on. But she did know that Magnus, her grandfather, was seething with rage.

#

Magnus and Draxon met at the bottom of the stairs. Soon Eren joined them. She had been crying and didn't have any words for her father or her fiancé.

"Eren, what's wrong?" Draxon asked, craning his neck to look at the tablet she was reading from, her hands shaking.

Moments after Draxon read what was written on the screen, it broke from the pressure he was putting on it after he had grabbed it to double check what he saw the first time.

Magnus watched them both, unsure what was happening.

"Eren did some checks," Draxon explained. "The fiend who did this to Dean... We found skin samples and bodily fluids, all preserved in jars in his room. We also found a Syndicate communicator. They've already taken six of our students since he started at the academy eight years ago. All Verantian children, all boys, all thirteen years old." Draxon looked at the floor, his face pale, and his eyes black.

Eren almost broke into tears again, her hands over her mouth.

Draxon handed the tablet back to her.

"Take some time, both of you," Magnus said. "I'll get Ellie to take Dean's work to him. We'll make sure this doesn't beat him, even if I have to do my own experiments."

He stormed away. Once he was out of sight of the others, he gave a loud scream of rage.

#

Dean's tears puddled on the floor all the way from his room to the lab, which was sealed while it was being investigated.

Draxon was sitting with Ellie and Ju Lan in Ellie's room looking at the trail of tears he knew lead back to a room filled with things no one wanted to see. "When the final report came in," he said, "Magnus was quoted by one of the bridge crew as having cursed the gods and having made a promise to a long-dead admiral."

"I… I can't believe that happened… to him, of all people. I should… I should say I'm here for him," Ellie said, standing up.

"He knows, he knows. Just focus on your tests and lessons. I'm sure he'll be alright."

Draxon left, the door shutting with a pressurised gulp.

"To suffer a scar not visible or physical and still continue on is the bravest act of all. Those who fight on, whether they want to or not, those whose deeds benefit others, not just themselves, are the true victims of war, for they are the ones who will never recover."

– Colonel Isnteba Ranfusbr, *History of Mental Illness in War* by Draxon Black

Chapter Nine: Nice Try, Ivanova

About a month passed, making a total of six months at the Academy. Dean maintained his distance from the others, in his isolation earning another two ranks, having reached Cadet Lieutenant Colonel, and achieving the reward for highest cadet rank in Academy history, as well as some of its best marks.

In the evenings he trained with his rifle. He had been asked by Magnus to listen to reports from the fifth city, most of which reminded him constantly of the horrors running around below. He would shoot in the furthest range from his room, with the reports playing in the background. His shooting benefited from it: he became less jumpy and learned to control his fear and anger in the moment, transferring any uncontrollable flinches to his left leg.

He made sure to fix the problems with the SMG and then tested it. His total range time exceeded even Draxon's.

Dean sometimes saw Draxon at the shooting range.

"Back again, Dean?" Draxon asked as he took out one of his pistols and started unloading down the range.

"All due respect, I didn't leave," Dean replied as he reloaded his rifle and took aim.

"Hold it." Draxon put the safety glass down, then walked into the range to retrieve his target. He looked at Dean's target, which was shredded, only the white outline remained. "Want me to replace yours? I think it's dead," Draxon said, laughing. Having received a nod from Dean, Draxon took his own target and then replaced Dean's, then returned to the shooting line and raised the glass. "Your test results keep coming back. It's amazing... You just keep breaking the bar," Draxon said as he inspected the twelve bullet holes in his target, which had a grouping of 0.002 millimetres.

"I just do my work as I'm told to," Dean said. "Well... I may throw in some other things. I believe you marked me quite low on my paper about the first three years of the Perpetual War."

Draxon smiled. "Not at all. I just deducted points for your opinionated response to question eighty-three." Draxon tucked his target into a pouch on his belt.

"Sorry Draxon, but could you put my gear away? The girls will be here soon and I'm not ready to talk to them yet."

Draxon held out his hand. Dean sighed, retrieved a small coin from his pocket, then handed it to Draxon.

"No problem, cadet. Maybe I got your gear out myself just to see if you were cleaning it," Draxon said before continuing to shoot.

Dean left, narrowly and avoided the girls.

"Draxon, how do we keep missing him?" Ellie demanded.

Draxon laughed. "Every time you are on your way here, Eren or Magnus appear, right?" he asked, putting his pistol on the table.

"Most of the time," Ju Lan said, the disappointment clear on her face. "This time it was Asmodeus."

"My god, you girls really do love him—" Draxon began.

Ellie cut him off with a glare. "Mind what you say, Commander. As for my grandfather and aunt, if they continue to keep me from my *friend*, I'll start a coup d'état."

With that, Ellie left. Ju Lan waved to Draxon, then followed her.

"Gah... if only they knew how he felt," Draxon said to

himself as he looked down the range.
He picked up his pistol quickly and fired a single round directly into the centre of the target.

#

Towards the end of the month, Draxon turned up at Dean's door. Beside him were Ellie and Ju Lan, who were both beaten and bruised – Ellie more so than Ju Lan. They both had black eyes and bruises around their necks, the marks of large hands.

"Dean, these two will be returning to your quarters. They are out of control, Lieutenant Colonel – you had better rein them in before I do." Draxon pushed the girls in before closing the door as fast as he could.

Dean barely looked over his tablet, but his silver eyes met those of both girls, who appeared at once ashamed and proud of the state they were in.

"You two seem pretty banged up," he said. "What happened?"

The room was exactly as they had left it. The bed frame still held their makeshift sleeping bags and their spare clothes were still neatly folded in the open drawers.

Dean was no thinner than before, and tucked behind the

bed was gym equipment to keep him in shape. He had weights, a treadmill to run on and a music player. Neatly laid out on his desk were a pot, kettle, and clean cutlery with a napkin folded underneath.

Both girls sensed that something had changed in him. As he took a deep breath, a slight smile crawled onto his face, and a tear clung to the inside of his eye.

"Some of the cadets were mouthing off about you," Ju Lan said. "Rumours, mostly, but one of them knew about your previous attempt on your life and made a guess that you had taken your life properly this time."

Ellie remained silent.

Dean swiped up on his tablet. "Is that all?"

Ellie spoke up finally. "They joked about it... what happened to you. They said they'd weed out us other Verantians out the same way. Ju Lan followed my lead, but I punched first. If you need to punish anyone... punish me."

Dean just smiled, then stepped forward and pulled them into a hug. "Thank you... both of you. Now I believe you might have some names?"

Ellie didn't' reply. She just held onto Dean, keeping him close to her.

Ju Lan smiled and winked as she backed away. "Corporals Vicia and Escaloni... both recently promoted, like many others – including yourself, Lieutenant Colonel

Ivanova. Nice one, sir."

Dean's badge lay on his desk along with the certificate he'd received. His other badges were in a pile behind the computer, along with a stupid joke present from Draxon tucked in the corner: an inflatable pistol that barely kept itself inflated.

"What about you guys?" Dean pushed Ellie away slowly to look at her badge on the top left of her chest. He glanced at it only briefly, embarrassed at his action.

"Ellie is Cadet Captain and I'm Cadet First Lieutenant. Which might be at risk now." Ju Lan touched her badge gently, as if it might shatter.

"Not if I have anything to say about it" Dean picked up his tablet from the bed and walked out of the room, followed by both girls.

The moment the air of the corridor hit Dean, he stopped, stunned by the sudden yet slight change in temperature and the new lights he'd heard being installed that very morning. He took a deep breath, then set off again, his feet like rolling thunder in the speed and force that they hit the floor, his mind focused.

Dean walked with urgency, typing into his tablet as he went, and the girls struggled to keep up with his long strides. He went straight to the infirmary, where a nurse was tending to two large human boys, the same two from the shuttle.

"I hear you're talking about me behind my back," Dean said. "Making threats to my friends'.' He handed his tablet to the nurse, who looked at the screen, then ran out of the room.

Ellie took a peek at the tablet as the nurse threw it down. It seemed standard, other than the case and screen protector, which had been made specially for Dean. In the corner of the screen was text that read simply, *Get Draxon and Magnus*. It was clearly part of Dean's plan, but Ellie wondered why he needed to ask for them.

"Yeah, so what?" Vicia said. "You're so weak, you let yourself get—"

He didn't finish his sentence. Dean punched the boy directly above the nose, knocking him unconscious and cracking his knuckles in the process. He left his hand there for a few seconds, his stance long as if he were trying to make himself smaller and harder to hit, yet giving himself more reach than he would normally have.

Dean turned to the quivering Escaloni and got right up in his face. When he spoke, his whisper was like nails on a chalkboard. "Now, Corporal. When your friend wakes, I want you to give him this message, and the same message goes for anyone. If you want to joke around and insult me, that's perfectly fine, go right ahead. If you dare insult, joke about, or threaten my friends, my race or my family, I will have no choice but to put you down. Do I make myself clear?" He stared into Escaloni's eyes, making the human boy quiver with fear.

"Understood, sir... Won't happen again, sir..." Escaloni said. His black eye and cuts were worse than anything the girls had sustained.

"Whilst I've got you in an intuitive mood, do you care to drop the reports about my friends, maybe forget who you picked a fight with?" Dean smiled and leant on the bed, cracking the knuckles of his other hand.

Escaloni nodded rapidly, then the lump of a boy fainted.

Dean turned and left, taking his tablet with him.

As he and the girls left the room, the nurse returned with Draxon, but they were too late to catch the trio – they only registered three students running away. As Dean turned the corner, he and Draxon exchanging brief grins.

"Dean, you didn't need to do..." Ellie began.

Dean stopped and grabbed both their hands. "You two have been kind, thoughtful and supportive towards me from day one. Let's not forget patient. Putting you two ahead of me is the least I can do. Now, how about we go curl up in our sheets and watch the stars?"

He held the girls' hands all the way back to their room, and they did indeed sit and watch the stars, though Dean soon fell asleep.

"Do you think he intended... romance?" Ju Lan asked, looking at Ellie other over the head of the sleeping boy between them.

"No, but if he did, it was a nice try... it'll take more than handholding, though." Blushing, Ellie resumed watching the stars.

"You held onto him for a good while when we first entered. Something you wanna say?"

Ellie wept silently for a while. "I failed to stop him from killing himself once. If it weren't for his powers, he'd be lost to us... I was just glad I didn't fail again." She wiped her eyes and turned to see Ju Lan doing the same.

Ju Lan smiled behind her hands. "Nice try, Ivanova – I know you're awake."

Dean opened his eyes.

"I'm sorry, guys... I needed time away from everyone to think. Say, Ellie, I'd like to meet your dad at some point. You too, Ju. I'd love to meet your family."

Ellie nodded before returning her eyes to the stars.

Ju Lan shook her head. "My family is died when I was young. A Syndicate sympathiser killed them during the riot a few years back. But I guess you could meet my foster parents."

Dean took her hand. "I'm sorry, Ju." He held her hand

and began tapping on his tablet with his other hand.

"What about your parents and brother?" Ellie said to Dean. "I'd love to meet them."

Dean and stopped tapping. "I'm not going home at the end of this year. I've booked extra classes and even signed myself up as mission ready. As for classes... Magnus deems it suitable for me to continue here... away from the hostility." He stood and entered the bathroom, using the toilet and then washing his hands and face.

He turned to see Ellie and Ju Lan standing in the doorway.

"Nice try, Ivanova, but if you don't return to classes we'll start attacking teachers next." Ellie said smiling a mean smile.

"Then ask to stay here – but in this classroom you have to teach yourself... teachers rarely come by except for the physical tests."

Dean went to leave the bathroom but they stopped him.

"Nice try Ivanova," Ju Lan said, "but you're coming back to class. Stop being a coward." She pushed them both out before closing the door.

They sat watching the stars for a few more hours. Even when they saw a couple of shooting stars, none of them spoke until Dean got up to go to sleep.

When he woke, both girls were once again sleeping next to him. He looked at both girls, but his gaze moved to Draxon, who was sitting on the chest of drawers, typing on his tablet. The flashes of the camera eventually woke Ellie too.

Ellie and Ju Lan moved into the corner, embarrassed and covering their vest tops and pyjamas with the sheets. Dean stood up.

"When Magnus wakes to see these photos, you had better hope that cadet camp's training is good enough," Draxon said with a smile.

Dean laughed. "For a teacher, you're mighty criminal."

As Dean approached, Draxon indicated to the door and they left the room together.

"Dean, are you alright?" Draxon asked. "Are you sure you don't need more time?"

"I'm not alright. I won't be alright. But I will be going back to class. Not for me, but for them." Dean pointed to his room. Dean removed his shirt, showing cuts and scars to show Draxon the truth.

Draxon inspected the cuts and scars. "What the hell did you use? These aren't clean." He ran his finger down the longest scar.

Dean's torso was covered in massive deep cuts and scars. It looked as though he'd been scratched by a tiger or a lion.

He was absolutely torn and looked like he might fall to bits at any moment.

Dean buttoned up his shirt. "I use whatever is at hand. But I'll stop if you just tell me one thing."

Draxon crossed his arms and looked at the door, trying not to let Dean see his anger. "What do you want to know?"

Dean looked at the door as well. "Ellie, Ju Lan, me – if you were ordered to... would you kill us?"

"Dean... you're asking a very difficult question. It shouldn't come to that... don't *make* it come to that. But if you're asking whether Magnus will order that attack... no. So when you think about it, you have nothing to worry about." He pushed the door to find both Ellie and Ju Lan standing directly behind it.

They had been using a glass to listen at a small crack in the door held open with Dean's dinner knife.

"I knew that would be the answer," Dean said. He went inside and closed the door.

Ellie watched Dean move to the centre of the room. "Dean, you don't have to protect us... we don't have to fear Draxon."

"I trust you two. Asmodeus too, at a stretch, but no one else. So here, let me show you Draxon's concerns."

When Dean removed his shirt, both girls took a step back. They looked him over for a few minutes in shock, stammering, trying to get words out, but no sound could be generated – not even when Ellie noticed the scar on Dean's back that had smaller scars splitting from it.

"Dean... what did you do? Why?" Ellie asked, running her hands over his scars.

Ju Lan walked into the bathroom.

"To make sure I'm still alive. Every night... I cut myself. The big one was first... I slipped showering, trying to get clean – but I can't feel clean. I can never feel clean." Dean took hold of Ellie's wrists and moved them away from him.

"Bullshit. Tell me... what can I do?" Ellie tried to put her hands on his shoulders, but he refused to let her.

"You can do everything you already do. That's enough for me."

Dean and Ellie stood struggling for a minute.

"What about the others – what can they do?" Ellie gestured to the bathroom with her head.

"You and Ju can do nothing more than you already do... I don't care about anyone else."

They kept struggling until they tripped over the bed, Ellie landing on top of Dean. They stayed there for a few minutes, just staring, each as red as the other.

When Ellie's tablet went off, she rushed up to check it. Ju Lan had been watching them, a large smile on her face.

"Oh god, no..." Ellie muttered. "Please, not now..." She

began to pace up and down.

Dean rushed to put his shirt back on.

"Ellie, what's wrong?" Ju Lan asked, approaching her.

Ellie handed her the tablet. "My father has decided to pay me a visit." She put her hands over her face.

Dean tucked in his shirt, then hugged her.

"He can't be that bad can he? What's his name? Thomas right? A psychologist?" Ju Lan said. She typed something on Ellie's tablet, then smirked. "Say what you want about your father, girl... he is *hot*." Ju Lan out got her own tablet and started looking at images.

"That's my problem. He's flashy, rude, inconsiderate – and the last time he met my sister's friends, he slept with them," Ellie stated.

This caught Ju Lan's attention. "You think he'll sleep with me?" she said excitedly, as if the prospect was too much to think about.

"God, no! My sister and her friends are fifty years old – or they were when he slept with them." Ellie let go of Dean and started pacing again.

"Yeah... Well, if I'm being honest, he might be good for someone in this room. Isn't your dad like a therapist or something?" Both Ju Lan and Ellie looked at Dean, who quickly picked up on what they were saying.

"Guys, I don't need a therapist," he said, rubbing his

shoulder.

"You don't want one, but you definitely need one," Ju Lan said. She smiled. "As for anything else, you did say you wanted to meet him."

Ellie bit down on her thumb.

They bickered about Ellie's father for a while, neither party having any intention of letting the other win.

Then it was too late. A white light appeared outside the window, quite far away. It got closer and closer until the vessel came into view. It was a small shuttle, painted white and gold with a giant phoenix on it. It looked like it cost as much, if not more than the entire Academy.

Ellie watched the shuttle enter the hangar bay. "That's his shuttle – Verula, he calls it. It means 'beauty' in Verantian... I hate it so much, you know, he spent more on that shuttle than everything I've ever owned. I own an entire moon and it still doesn't compare to that piece of shit."

"If you guys want to go greet him, I'll be fine," Dean said slightly nervous. He went into the bathroom and waited for the outer door to open and close.

But it didn't.

"Dean," Ellie said, "I barely want to see the man myself.

Why would I ditch you when I can just sit here and chat with you instead?"

Her tablet went off again.

"It doesn't sound like your grandfather plans on letting you just sit and chat," Dean said. He left the bathroom, blood soaking into the shoulder of his shirt.

"You've reopened one of your cuts," Ellie said. "Ju, go get a medical kit from the infirmary. If you see my dad, stall him. Sleep with him if you have to."

She removed Dean's shirt and sat him down, getting a clean pair of socks and wetting one to dab at the cut.

Ju Lan left the room without argument. The smile on her face was almost impossible to miss. She had rushed out so fast she had forgotten to put boots on and ended up slipping down the top stairs with an excited shriek.

Dean sat on the bed frame as Ellie began to clean his wound with a wet black sock, but his scar wouldn't stop bleeding.

He stared out the window and smiled, almost laughing.

Ellie checked all of his cuts. His back was covered in blood.

"What's so funny?" she asked.

"The last words my mother said to me before I left the house at two in the morning. 'You find yourself a nice girl and you hope she changes you.' Little did she know I'd have two good friends looking after me."

Ellie used the dry sock to soak up blood. "Your dad a military man?"

She wanted to keep Dean talking, because she'd left the sock on too long and the blood had caused it to start sticking, as Dean noticed as she picked at the sock with a fork.

"Yeah..." he said. "His dad, too. My father's line has been military since we were clans roaming over Verantia Prime... Damn shame my brother can't sign up. He was the soldier, not me. Sure, I was strong, competitive and a martial arts king – but he had a head for tactics... I'm just an animal fighting his own instincts." He looked up at the window, wincing every time Ellie pulled a strand of the now butchered sock from his scarred back.

The door shot open and Dean heard angry footsteps, followed by the pitter patter of small feet in socks.

Ju Lan, Magnus, and a red-haired man wearing white clothes stood at the door. Both Magnus and the newcomer appeared completely shocked by Dean's scars.

"Fuck." Dean went to get up, but Ju Lan put the medic kit next to him and kept him sitting by tapping his shoulders where his two most recent scars were located.

"Sorry guys, I tried my best... but he's the headmaster." Ju Lan took over from Ellie, who looked straight past Magnus at the other man.

"Well, Father, as you can see I'm quite busy. So tell me what you want and then I can—"

Ellie was cut off by Magnus, who stepped forward and moved her aside to look Dean in the eye.

Dean looked straight down. He could feel Magnus's burning gaze on his torso. Magnus moved around him, studying his cuts and scars, choosing his words.

"What the fuck did you do to yourself?" Magnus said finally.

Dean didn't look up. "After the... after the incident, I started to feel empty... like nothing. The first cut was from slipping whilst getting out of the large bath and shower in that ridiculously large bathroom. The rest are all self-inflicted."

Ellie and Ju Lan wrapped bandages around his shoulders and back. After they had finished, a different cut reopened and they moved to deal with that.

"Why?" Magnus asked, swallowing his emotions to stare coldly through the window, .

Dean shot to his feet, pulling Ellie with him. "To see if I was still worth something, if I could still bleed after what was done to me!"

He caught Ellie with one arm and helped her back to a stable footing. Ellie put one hand on his shoulder and the other on his chest. She blushed, then continued with the bandaging.

"Father, could you take Cadet First Lieutenant Lan for a walk about," Thomas said. "I would like to have a conversation with Cadet Lieutenant Colonel Ivanova and my daughter." He stepped out of the way to let the others leave before he closed the door.

"Ellie, my dear," he said. "Could you heat up that large needle in hot, clean water, please?"

He knelt behind Dean, whose fists clenched as he sat back down.

"Dean?" the man said. "Can I call you Dean? I'm going to need to seal up this particular cut. Unfortunately, you've done some real damage, but the scars will make you look particularly manly later on,"

Thomas Phoenix muttered as he put his hand gently on Dean's shoulder.

"I'd prefer Ellie do it... I've had enough old men standing behind me to last me a lifetime," Dean said jokingly, only to feel a burning pain seconds later. A bright golden light erupted from Thomas's hand and Dean yelled out in pain.

Ellie rushed back in and pushed her father away from Dean, who remained where he was. His cut had burned shut.

"What was the fucking idea there, Dad? Burn him to

death?" Ellie inspected the sealed cut to make sure not too much damage had been done – but Dean's body was healing quickly.

"Ellie, my dear, you overreact. But since you're in such an energetic mood, I thought you should know. I have chosen someone for—"

Ellie punched her dad square in the teeth.

"I will not be forced into a marriage the moment I turn sixteen," she said. "I will not perpetuate this misogynistic cycle of bullshit. I am a soldier. The only men who tell me what to do are my superiors."

She walked out, calm and collected – but the atmosphere she had left behind was anything but collected.

"Sir," Dean said, "thank you for the medical aid. If you would like me to stop sleeping next to your daughter in return, I will oblige... although begrudgingly."

He turned around to put on a clean shirt.

Thomas wiped the blood from his split lip. "Please. I want to let her marry on her own. If she wants to sleep next to you, do so. I'm only here because I have to tell her that my father has decided her husband."

Dean swivelled around. "You mean Magnus?"

"Yes... our great king." Thomas stood up and brushed himself down. "Honestly, I'd rather have nothing to do with the girl... a whore's product is what she is. That pain I put you through, all to spite her. A whore in the making."

Thomas had only just seen Dean's fists clench before Dean smashed the computer. Thomas looked at the boy like he was insane – then he laughed. "I don't believe it!? You're in love with the little whore!" He laughed even louder.

Dean became angrier still, until he snapped. He jumped over the bed frame and tackled Thomas, striking the three-thousand-year-old and pulling no punches. He was so furious he let out a scream before lifting Thomas onto his shoulder and charging at the wall with him. They went crashing through the metal wall and ended up standing in front of Eren and Draxon.

Dean was striking Thomas relentlessly, and the man could barely get an arm up to defend himself, but finally he kicked Dean away. Dean hit the wall but charged right back in.

This time they went over the railing of the stairs, landing directly in front of Ellie. Thomas had landed on his back but Dean was on his feet, having twisted his ankle but managing to stay standing. He charged again, but Thomas pushed him away with his legs before standing up. This didn't last long, though: Dean looked to his left and picked up a trash bin that had been bolted down, and threw it directly at Thomas, who dropped to the floor to dodge the metal box filled with ration pack drinks and packets.

Eren and Draxon came bounding down the stairs, but they were too late. Dean was at Thomas's throat, not letting up and beating the man easily, until Magnus interfered. He split the two brawlers apart as easily as he might pluck a leaf from a tree, then approached them, looking disapprovingly at Draxon, who was being held back by Eren.

"What in the name of the homeworld are you two idiots doing? Do you know how hard you have to tackle someone to break through eight inches of steel?"

Dean was still trying to get at Thomas.

"Father," Thomas said, holding his broken nose. "I don't know what you're teaching these kids, but for a boy thirteen years old to know this much violence... shame on you."

Dean spat blood.

During the argument, Eren muttered under her breath about the difference between the Galactic and planetary calendars.

"I'm more disappointed in the shit parenting job he did," Dean said. "For you to call your own daughter a whore – you disgust me. You betray everything it means to be Verantian. My parents fought biology itself to have my brother, and you, who impregnated Ellie's mother and called them both whores... you're not royal. I'd strip you of your powers if I could."

Dean felt Magnus relax, although the heat he was emitting made Dean step back.

Magnus stood Dean up straight, then looked at Thomas. His face sunken with fear, as if he knew what would happen next.

"Thomas Aurelius Phoenix. Did you say those awful things about your own daughter and wife, only to get beaten up by a child?"

Magnus put his hand on Dean's shoulder. Dean could still feel the heat but it wasn't scorching him.

"Sir, if I may..." Draxon said, "why not consult the recordings from Dean's room?" He stepped forward to hand his tablet to Magnus. He was still being held back by Eren with all her strength, but only by the belt.

Magnus watched the last few months of recordings, looking up at Dean each time Dean, Ellie and Ju Lan went to sleep. Dean gulped, but Draxon laughed every time it happened. Eren relaxed, falling to her knees in exhaustion. Eventually Magnus reached the point he was looking for, and he listened using a single earpiece device. He listened to every word, his teeth grinding when Dean was burned, and his hair and eyes lighting up as if they were on fire when Thomas uttered the words he had so carelessly thrown around.

Everyone saw the anger in Magnus's eyes. The tablet melted into a puddle of metal and glass, which cooled and went hard, forming a pile of junk that served no other purpose than to mark the spot where a father and son had their family bond stripped away.

Eren jumped to her feet and backed away, dragging Dean and Draxon with her. Draxon reacted physically to the tug, grabbing the corner of the wall to remain standing. Dean wasn't so lucky: he fell flat on his arse with Eren tugging him back to his feet as Magnus started to move.

"Thomas Phoenix, I hereby strip you of your rank and your family name and cast you from your culture. Your powers are forfeit and your assets will go to the two injured parties. I also banish you from this station and all Varantian-controlled space."

As Magnus put his hand out, Thomas's eyes turned a normal brown colour. His hair colour faded and he began to age slightly.

Unbeknownst to the angry king, students, teachers, and security had gathered at the doors of the classrooms and the canteen to watch. Some of the older students, who wore kit similar to Draxon's and the security officers, had even started filming or taking photos. One girl focused not on Magnus but Draxon, who noticed and whispered to Eren.

Draxon and two guards rushed Thomas away from the growing crowed as he screamed and cursed, crying like a spoiled child, "Father, no! Give me my birthright back! Mother, Mother, help me! Tell him, tell him!" But his screams were drowned out as he was taken to the pod room.

"Dean Ivanova," Magnus said, "you have protected the honour of my family, the honour of my daughter and, most importantly, the honour of this school. I hereby grant you the power taken from the criminal scum Thomas, and hope you use them better." Again, he raised his hand, palm down. Dean's silver eyes glowed a bit brighter and his veins turned gold.

"Magnus... sir..." Dean began, "I'm sorry about the wall and about all the trouble. Please, I insist you take my rank from me and punish me."

Magnus only shook his head. "The only punishment I see fit to give you would also punish two others, so I cannot do that. But as of tomorrow you will return to classes, and you will stop self-harming. After your lessons you'll report to my office under the main control room."

Magnus started to walk away, then turned around to look at everyone else. "*What?* Are you all going to stand there gawking or are you going to *get back to class?*" He waited for everyone except Dean, Eren and Ellie to leave before walking away, his footsteps heavy and his hands in his pockets, his head hung low to look at the floor.

"Dean, are you okay?" Ellie rushed over and looked him over, hugging him after confirming there was nothing wrong.

"Dean," Eren said, "I would like to ask you something in private. Could you step in here please?" She guided Dean from the once more gathering crowd and into a maintenance closet.

Dean sat down on a stepping stool clutching his ribs. "What did you want to ask me, Eren?"

"Would you be willing to lead a team back to the fifth city? As punishment?"

Dean's pain left him, only to be replaced with fear.

#

"A superior who punishes their troops with the next fight is the only superior to truly do what it takes. But a soldier who agrees despite their fear is the true leader of the battlefield."

– High King Sylvester S. Sortovenic, *The King in Black and White* by Draxon Black and Magnus Phoenix

Chapter Ten: The First City's Destruction

Draxon and Eren's bedroom was just along the hall from Dean's. Their room was smaller than his, and they crammed themselves into a small double bed that Draxon alone barely fit into, leaving Eren sprawled out over him. Their room would normally be quiet enough to hear a pin drop, but tonight the air left everything out of place, and a space that normally would be serene and silent became a vortex of memories and misfortune.

Draxon woke from sleep, sweating and struggling to breathe. As he got up to get a glass of water, Eren, who was asleep next to him, rolled over onto his side of the bed and spread out.

Draxon smiled briefly. His breathing was still hard and sweat drenched his long johns.

"Magnus... what the hell are you thinking? Sending that boy back down..." In the bathroom, Draxon leant on the sink and looked into the mirror, remembering the first time he had been afraid of loss – the day the Verantian Monarchy lost the most of its soldiers and its nobles.

#

Twenty years prior

Draxon ran through the blood-covered corridors of the large hotel, the type that stood in the centre of every city of the afflicted colonies. He checked each open door and found only carnage.

Eventually, after climbing fifty-eight floors, he arrived at the ladder leading to the roof. He climbed it slowly, leaving his shotgun at the bottom to avoid being encumbered. He peeked out of the hatch. Zombies had surrounded the large VIP cage, a metal and glass bird cage like structure that stood tied onto the top of the hotel tower.

When he had first arrived, the cage had been full of rich men and women awaiting rescue. Now it contained Eren, her soldiers and ten of the ten thousand survivors they had rescued, all moving heavy furniture onto the hatch inside the cage.

Draxon looked around to check the area was clear, but as he was about to go up he was dragged back down the ladder by small, blood-covered hands. They belonged to a soldier he and Eren had been training with, a girl Draxon had chosen specifically for the mission. Half her face was missing and she was covered in teeth marks. Her insides were ripped and torn and she was pale from blood loss.

Draxon fought to keep her from biting him and prevent her long nails and teeth from scratching at him. He looked at the ladder and the shotgun, but he was stuck under the girl.

She noticed the shotgun too, and fought ever harder to keep Draxon down, eventually driving her left hand into his stomach nails first, puncturing right through his clothes and his flesh. She bit into his right arm and shoulder, pulling away massive chunks as she drove her hand deeper and deeper.

In a last-ditch effort, Draxon drew his pistol and shot through himself, catching the shoulder and chest of the girl, who only bit harder. Draxon shot until his pistol was empty, the very last round hitting the girl in the head.

As he lay bleeding to death, Draxon noted the peaceful expression of his former comrade. He began to cry from the pain due to the thirty small holes, and the large hole from his dead friend's hand.

He dragged himself across the floor to grab the 12-gauge shotgun, then climbed the ladder using his good arm.

Slowly, he told himself. *What if I'm too late? What if they've killed her. I can't lose her. I won't lose her. Faster, faster, faster. Move faster!*

His eyes turned completely black as he burst through the hatch. Once he was on the roof he pulled the shotgun from under his arm and unleashed the first slug into the crowd of flesh eaters.

As they turned to face him, he threw the shotgun up and caught the pump bar, letting gravity pull the gun down before throwing it back up to catch the handle and fire another slug at another zombie.

He did this a total of six times until the shotgun clicked, its chamber empty.

Draxon threw the shotgun at a zombie and pulled out his second pistol, which he used to take out another thirty zombies. With his pistols and shotgun empty, he unclipped his rifle and emptied the seventy-round magazine into the horde of dead humans.

He'd cut their numbers in half but now he was out of ammo, and they were coming for him.

He fought them back with the short combat knife, which he'd ripped from its pouch before he'd even had a second to think. The knife had a divot cut into it, so that it went in with a clean cut, but on its way out it would tear and ruin the target.

The zombies seemed wary of him, as if they had maintained some level of intelligence that Draxon and the others had overlooked.

As he stood fighting with one arm, bullets tore through the zombies from one side. Five hundred feet away was the WarHawk, having bided its time and slaughtered the rest of the zombies.

Draxon smiled as he fell backwards, his vision going black.

#

He was brought back around in the bathroom by Eren's cold hands slipping across his scarred skin. The bite marks and missing chunks were scarred, but not as badly as he might have expected. The hole in his stomach looked like a star in the sorts of movies filmed with far too much lens flare.

"What's got you so worried?" Eren asked. "Normally you don't wake up unless something terrible bothers you."

Draxon looked at her in the mirror. She was wearing a red nightdress, her hair down and flowing over her shoulders. "It's Dean," he said. "This challenge your father came up with, it's not right."

"It needs to be done, Draxon. It's not just a test of Dean but all of them. The Emperor is crunching down on us hard, and we need to prove our cadets are ready, even if the first year omits combat training from the curriculum. My dad is just doing as he's told."

Eren stroked Draxon's right shoulder and kissed his neck.

"I still don't agree. Even if his eyes are special, there's no reason to test him like this. Even my test wasn't this bad, and you had to figure out if I was insane or not."

Draxon put his hand over Eren's and pulled her up his back gently. She wrapped her legs around his waist and her arms around his neck and shoulders, resting her head on the back of his own.

"At least Dean has you, and Ellie and Ju Lan," she said. "We didn't give you that luxury. We made sure you had no friends. We made sure you were alone. I'm just glad you confronted me that day."

Eren clung onto Draxon as he returned to the bedroom.

"I had to," he said. "You were too busy trying to impress... whatever that rich kid's name was." He laid Eren gently on the bed, struggling to recall people from his past.

"Yes – Evican. Don't remind me of that," Eren said, and laughed.

Draxon smiled and sat down. "What happened to him?"

Eren thought for a second. "He was in the first city. He died. As did his brother and father, and half the noble families. Half the mansions built on our new homeworld are empty, or widows with no heirs. There are so few of us left in the centre of the galaxy..." She looked at the floor.

Draxon stood and got dressed. "I'll be back," he said.

He kissed Eren on the forehead before leaving the bedroom, at which point he bumped into two senior cadets who were kissing.

"So you decided to stand outside the teachers' rooms and our pets? Couldn't you two use your heads? Detention, the both of you – *separate* detentions. Now head back to your dorms before I wake up the headmaster and have him give you a bollocking."

Draxon ushered the two students away, then headed downstairs and into the familiar, ghostly quiet corridors. He walked every corridor of the silent halls of the Academy and he checked every classroom, the canteens, and the kitchens. He moved as quietly as the night, and eventually he arrived at the door to the armoury, which was open, the guard asleep against the wall.

Draxon looked around the large vault door to see Dean tinkering with some of the weapons, his rifle and sword resting in the corner. As he watched, Dean reached for a backpack tearing one of his cuts open and staining his white shirt red.

"Bit late to be checking inventory, isn't it, Dean?" Draxon said with a smile.

"Just making sure we have everything ready before we go back. It won't only be me and the girls – I have a whole team to take care of. I wanna get as much out of the way as possible." Dean filled the bag with ammo and weapon attachments before reaching for another one, which he filled with medical supplies.

"Let me be clear, Dean. They will say there is no support. You must *believe* there is no support. But the moment things get too much, I will be coming. I've lost a lot of people to this parasite, and I refuse to lose more."

Draxon stopped Dean from continuing with his work. He opened one of the medkits and bandaged Dean up.

Dean sighed. "Did Eren mention that Magnus had her ask me?" He looked over his shoulder at Draxon, who broke the lid off the medkit in shock.

"No. But I knew she had a hand in planning it." Draxon slid the medkit to the corner of the room and picked up Dean's equipment starting with Dean's prototype rifle, which he began to service.

"Don't get me wrong," Dean said, "it's a good plan. But the briefing materials... the reports... not even a full contingent could complete this mission." He looked at the rifle, his hand shaking as he remembered the night he was attacked.

"You can't truly believe that a contingent of humans is worth anywhere near you and the girls." Draxon smiled. "Forget the rest. I'd rather have you three cadets come to back me up, no matter the situation."

Dean laughed. "You're just saying that because you want me to feel more confident." He smiled watching as a small spider-like creature scurried up a dust-covered box.

"Do you even realise how well you three are doing?" Draxon took his mini tablet out of his pocket and scrolled until he found Dean's file. "Dean Ivanova. Mentally sturdy when given something to protect, and strong at all times. His mental capabilities are beyond that of most third-year students and seem to improve with every obstacle he faces. In turn he has inspired many students to try that little bit harder. As for his grades, considering the fact that he has spent a good portion of his time in his room and not actually in class, he has some of the best, if not *the* best grades across all subjects. And here it says we must keep you at all costs," Draxon concluded, before looking up from his screen at Dean

Dean was still watching the spider, which was spinning itself into a small home. "Can I be honest with you, Draxon?" he asked.

"Always."

Dean took out a pocket watch and showed Draxon a picture of his father and mother.

"I don't know who my dad was," he said. "I told Ellie and maybe Ju Lan that he was military, but the truth is I don't know. I like to think it's because of him that I'm here, but I'm not sure."

He sighed as more spiders swarmed the house and made their own white homes.

"Whoever he was, I can happily say you are twice the man he was." Draxon handed the watch back. "Now, off to bed with you. I'll finish up here."

After Dean had left, Draxon remained sitting on the floor, cleaning the rifle. "Colnor, you alcoholic son of a bitch," he muttered. "You should never have gone without Magnus."

Later, when he had finished organising the stuff for Dean and was closing the armoury, Magnus came by, biting his fingernails.

"Ah, Draxon," he said. "Just the man I wanted to see. Look, I know you don't like it and I know there's nothing to say to *make* you like it, but Dean is ready for his final trial. He passed the first and second, even passing the trial that my son so idiotically provided. Now we just need him to pass this last trial and that's it, near normal education afterwards." As he spoke, Magnus bit each of his pinkie fingers in turn.

"Then why are you biting your nails?" Draxon asked.

Realising what he was doing, Magnus stopped. "It's Ellie. She may be doing well and she may have golden eyes... but she'll never be a proper soldier. She cares too much. I don't know what to do with her," he admitted.

Draxon laughed. "Magnus, you're like an estranged uncle to me. You can't stop her now. She's in deep. After she comes back – because she will – you might be able to convince her to leave. But until Dean's father returns, she's all the family he has."

Draxon sighed weakly and made to turn away, but Magnus stopped him. "He has you and Eren," he said with a sigh. "He looks up to you both. Ellie is like Eren – gung-ho and emotionally driven. Not to mention completely unlike a princess . You're right. But you are also his family. We all are, now." Magnus walked off, one of his fingers bleeding.

Draxon looked at the vault door, then sighed and reopened it and began servicing weapons once more – not only Dean's and his own, but everyone else's as well. He started with the training weapons on the left of the locker, then moved slowly and surely to the live-action weaponry, all individually sealed behind metal cage doors, each weapon with its own code. Once he got to the end, he walked out and locked the vault.

He kicked the guard awake, then headed off. He stared at the door of a dorm room as he passed. It was sealed with a magnet and upon it were eight signs in different languages. The signs all said the same thing: *Keep Out – Danger*.

"Fucking zombies," Draxon muttered.

He kept walking, then eventually he settled on a small bench at the bottom of the stairs. The repairs as a result of Dean and Thomas's brawl had already been completed.

#

"During my long life, I have seen great good and great evil. All start the same, as a child going through some sort of education. What the students that I and others teach at the Academy will become is unknown to us – however, they will eventually make a decision about whether they want to be good or evil. I can only hope they make the choice that saves the most lives in the long run, as I have tried to do."

– Magnus Phoenix, *The Golden Phoenix* by Draxon Black

Chapter Eleven: Return to the Fifth City

A week passed, and every day Ellie apologised to Dean for her father's actions. She apologised in class, at lunch, before bed and after each point they were separated for more than a minute.

It got so bad that she would message him in class, asking if he hated her because of her father, then looked over at him. Each time, he sighed and responded in the same way: "No, I don't hate you. And you don't need to apologise."

One night as she was about to apologise, Dean snapped. "Look! Stop apologising. If I hated you, I wouldn't let you sleep next to me. In fact, I'd probably throw you out – quite literally. But I like you, sometimes more than I care to admit, so will you please just chill out?"

"I, uh... Okay. Just do me a favour and hold me a little closer tonight, so I don't cry," Ellie said as they entered his bedroom.

That night you wouldn't have been able to get a pinkie finger between them – and Ju Lan certainly tried. She had grown tired of how close they were becoming to one another.

The next morning, when Dean went to get changed, she pounced on Ellie. "Hey! You said we were doing this together! Stop hogging him. I feel bad, too."

Ellie just blinked at her friend. "Why? My father was the one who fucked up," she said in shock and disbelief that Ju Lan was so jealous of them.

"Maybe. But I was the one who wasn't strong enough to keep your dad and Magnus out of the way while you dealt with Dean. I could have led them anywhere, but I brought them straight here. If he hates anyone, it's me. The snitch." She was furious at herself and, somehow, at Ellie and Dean too.

Ellie simply laughed.

"*Hey!* This isn't funny! I'm serious!" Ju Lan yelled; her face going red.

Dean came out of the bathroom in a new shirt. "What's going on here? Did I interrupt something?" he asked, confused.

"Dean, you won't believe what Ju just said!" Ellie said, still laughing, trying to find something to hold onto to prevent herself from falling over.

Dean looked at them both. "What? It must be one hell of a joke."

Ju Lan was now getting angry at Dean, too. "Oi! I wasn't joking. I meant every word."

"She thinks she could have kept my father and grandfather from wandering around at ten in the morning on a Saturday," Ellie said, wiping tears of from her eyes and slumping against the chest of drawers. "You know, the day my aunt and grandfather told you that you had to make up for all the times you'd been let off the hook? She blames herself."

Dean turned to Ju Lan. "Ju, I thought you were the smart one. What happened was just the will of whatever cruel being guides our lives – or it was just bad luck. Take your pick. But none of it was your fault. In fact, I'm fully to blame. Now, since you seem to have knocked Ellie's legs out from under her, would you like to come grab some extra range time with me?"

When he held out his hand, Ju Lan pounced at him, grabbing his arm, and pulling him out the door before Ellie could recover.

After their session at the range, the pair sat down in the cafeteria to talk.

"Dean I was wondering..." Ju Lan began.

Dean smiled and sipped his drink. "Oh? Wondering what?"

"Where did you learn to shoot? To fight, and to... just... act so cool?" Ju Lan looked down at her cooling drink.

"When I was three," Dean began, "my mother let me meet my father for the first time. He said he had some sort of important mission, but before he went, he taught me the basics of shooting. My brother was only two, so he never got any training, Over the years, my mother enrolled me in every activity. At one point I heard the parents of one of my classmates chatting, and they said my father had left because he was embarrassed by me and my brother. So, I made it my mission to become the best. I trained every day and beat every opponent."

He was being brutally honest, and it was clear that he still experienced guilt.

"Dean, I..." Ju Lan wanted to say more, but she stopped, not knowing the words to use.

"Honestly, I enjoyed the journey," Dean said, "but I'm not sure how that makes me look. Also, I don't know truly how to act around people. I just want to make my dreams come true. Now I look at them through my own eyes. But I must also do what my brother wanted to do. Maybe one day he'll get better, but I truly doubt it." He finished his drink and stood up.

Ju Lan looked up at him. "Can I tell Ellie what you've told me?"

Dean nodded, then stretched. "I'm going to go find Draxon and get some extra command training before my punishment." He waved goodbye and then left the cafeteria.

#

At the end of the sixth week following Thomas's visit, Eren collected Dean, Ellie and Ju Lan from history class, and took them to the hangar, where a group of fifteen cadets had gathered,

Asmodeus among them.

"Attention!" Eren commanded in a loud voice summoned from the depths of her small frame.

All the cadets slammed their feet together in booming unison, looking straight ahead, ready for Eren's inspection.

Dean saluted the cadets, and they saluted him in return. He hadn't really thought about the Verantian salute much, but now it made sense to him. The feet were directly together, facing forward to symbolise the straight and narrow path every soldier walks upon. The right hand came up to cover the heart with a flat palm, to symbolise protection of the cadets themselves and those they loved, whilst the left hand rested upon the pistol holster to indicate readiness for battle.

"Listen up you pathetic imbeciles," Eren said. "Most of you are here because your grades are falling. Four of you are here because you volunteered, and one of you keeps breaking things. You now are locked in for this unsupervised mission. You will be led by Lieutenant Colonel Ivanova and his two girlfriends, Captain Phoenix, and First Lieutenant Lan. Now, I can make fun of them and call them his girlfriends because I am the aunt of one of them, and the teacher of the other. You are all shitters in comparison. You do not know them. You do not know your enemy. They do. I leave the rest to Commander Black to explain. He's waiting at the armoury. Go."

Everyone but Dean bolted.

Dean's eyes were locked on the door to the room where he was attacked, which still had tape over it to prevent people from entering, along with a barrier that seemed to get knocked every time someone passed it.

Dean could see the other mechanics were ashamed. Even now, none of them seemed to have any personality, and all of them avoided his eyes. The engineering students deliberately avoided him, and two even jumped railings to avoid him seeing them, though then the lift they had jumped onto rose into view and they stared at him awkwardly.

"You okay, Dean?" Eren asked, moving in front of him, blocking the door and demanding he focus on her.

He nodded. "Yeah... just thinking is all. Is that lab used now?" He pointed to the sealed doors. His hand was heavy and shaking slightly, and a scar from where he had been cut turned deep red as blood rushed from his hand.

Eren kept her eyes on him. "No. And you'll have to do something mighty impressive to convince my father to let you use it."

She had seen right through him. It made him smile. He thought of the others, all trying to get through the hangar doors at the same time. Ju Lan and Ellie just stood watching the others struggle, even though they had led the charge for a while.

"Alright," he said, "I'll bring everyone back alive and unharmed. I've got two reasons to fight for them now."

He turned and walked away, pushing through the crowd of cadets easily to be the first to reach the armoury.

He waited half an hour until everyone else arrived. He gave Ellie and Ju Lan disappointed looks that tore right through them, but then he smiled and winked at them, which made Ellie turn as red as a bell pepper.

He was given his kit, including the rifle and blade the Syndicate agent had made. He checked everything a few dozen times before falling in at the back alongside

Asmodeus.

"Are you doing alright, Lieutenant Colonel?" Asmodeus asked. He was carrying an LMG and a large bag. A few of his scales had lost their colour and he seemed to have a cold, which amused Dean slightly.

"I'm fine, Second Lieutenant Sniffles. I'm going to be counting on you down there. Tell me can you still shoot straight with that blocked nose?"

Asmodeus choked before speaking. "Of course, but let's be fair – if I open fire on them, it's only because you missed them," Asmodeus joked, producing a hissing, cold-ridden laugh.

"The Lieutenant Colonel will lead you all back to the hangar," Draxon announced. "You will load up on the WarHawk and it will drop you at the access gate to the fourth city. You will then make your way to the entrances to the sixth city and make sure they are all sealed before returning to the large central tower for extraction. This will not be easy. Some of you will die."

He nodded to Dean, who began to walk away along with everyone else. Dean's plan revealed to Draxon, probably by Eren, the pressure starting to weigh his broad shoulders down like a sack of bricks.

The walk to the WarHawk was long and silent, at least

for Dean and Ellie. Dean led the way with the prototype rifle and his sword, which bounced gently on his back.

Ellie walked slightly behind him, only by a little. TO an untrained eye she was stood beside him, hurrying constantly to keep up, as she was struggling with the rifle she had been given.

The rest of the group spoke to each other, with Ju Lan and Asmodeous talking quite loudly about Dean.

"Yeah I mean, he does have his issues – but we all do," Ju Lan said to Asmodeous in a playful tone. "Look at me – I got devolved. I'm just lucky enough to have survived it."

"Yeah, but you also seem to struggle with that rifle." Asmodeus said.

It was true that Ju Lan was suffering just like Ellie. "Yeah, well, I've only ever used an SMG," she replied. "You could say that small things suit me better, being on the petite side."

"You saying the Lieutenant Colonel doesn't have a large package, then?" Asmodeus said, trying not to smile.

Ju Lan took the bait. "No! I'm sure Dean has quite a large—" She stopped when everyone laughed.

At the front of the group, Dean went red.

"Uh huh... Well you should speak up next time," Asmodeus said calmly. "Range days are one thing, but as you well know, we can't risk being caught unaware."

The older students behind them were panicking silently.

Eren and two men in flight suits, who were standing talking by an uncovered WarHawk, noticed the students walking towards them. The men headed inside the small craft and Eren turned to face the cadets.

The jet was black with no windows. On its door and wings were a Phoenix symbol and seven numbers.

Dean put his arm out and everyone stopped. He walked over to Eren, who smiled. Then Dean took a closer look at the WarHawk now that it was unveiled.

It was a three-engine craft with the ability to rotate the two jets on its wings to hold itself in the air. The third engine was on the bottom of the main hull, the landing gear folding into small spaces on either side. It also had a ramp that could be used as a gunner port, with a medium bulletproof window.

The small doors on either side were pure metal. They were open, allowing a glimpse of the interior seats and metal conveyor like at the airports, but just in the floor.

"Lieutenant Colonel, is your squad ready?" Eren asked, saluting Dean.

He saluted in return. "Yes ma'am. Although I have a couple of concerns I'd like to discuss."

Eren dropped her salute, allowing Dean to do the same. "Tell me about them," she said. She crossed her arms, nodding to someone behind Dean.

Dean didn't turn around to look. "It's about extraction, and nothing else. But I don't think that extracting via the roof of a zombie-infested tower is the best idea... if we get trapped, we're done for. I'd rather exfil from the gates or a park." Dean let his rifle hang by his side as he spoke, his eyes telling her everything she needed to know, his fists clenched at his sides out of fear.

"Hmm. That's true, and from last reports, the shutters were all down and secure. I don't know any other way for you to extract." Eren pulled up a hologram of the fifth city. "The parks are all forested, with limited open space, and the sixth city gates are mostly underground."

Dean pointed to an area on the map. "What about the main intersection? That's large, and I suspect that the lampposts will be easy to topple, if they still remain standing. I walked through there on my little excursion. It's big enough for the WarHawk but would still be easy to defend using the buildings around it, although they're more like ruins."

Eren shook her head. "That's too far to go after closing the sixth city gates. Those tunnels will be dangerous. I mean, you might be able to use the rail network or maybe even the sewers to get around, but they both have their risks." She showed the tunnel entrance to the sixth city and the closest train station.

"No, the rail network was a monorail. It's not safe to walk on or even get close to. It and most structures will be crumbling." Dean stared at the map. "As for sewers... I get the feeling that when most people fled into them, more than a few infected went with them – or the zombies might have even gone after them. No, it's too much of a risk."

Surprised at his intellectual and strategically sound reasoning, Eren said, "Dean – no, Lieutenant Colonel – I can't offer you any better strategies than what we have at the moment. Maybe when you see how the situation has changed, you can come up with something. After all, we haven't sent anyone down there since our evacuation." She put away her tablet with a sigh.

"I'll figure it out. Wish us luck."

Dean saluted and called everyone forward with a single head movement.

He started loading everyone up the back ramp to sit in the seats.

When Dean noticed the large ammo crate, he pointed to it, making Eren laugh.

"It's a gift," she said. "More magazines, and close to the bottom is a piece of tech Magnus wants you to test."

Dean opened the crate and moved some stuff aside to find a large rifle with a box magazine, along with backpacks and a bomb.

The large rifle looked like it might weigh more than everything else in the box combined.

"Yup. I know just the man," Dean said. He closed the lid and clipped it down.

"Dean. On the side, there is an aspect both me and Draxon were curious about... We need you to check on the sewers – it's why I mentioned them. We picked up a life sign. It could be one of ours."

Dean who sighed and nodded before walking over to his seat. When he sat down, the ramp closed. The WarHawk lifted up and sped out of the hangar, making very little noise, but what noise it did make was similar to a jet engine, only so quiet that inside the craft it was completely silent and outside you could still talk with it fully throttled.

Ellie and Dean sat across from each other, just staring at one another. Ju Lan smiled jealously from the other end of the seats, and Asmodeus was laughing hysterically, before sneezing and sending clear white snot all over the feet of an older boy, who threw up on his own feet two seconds later.

The ride was very fast and smooth. The WarHawk entered the city dome after only seconds of travel. Given the twenty barrelled, high velocity, large calibre miniguns strapped to the front and wings of the craft, they were prepared to handle a small army.

"Lieutenant Colonel, this is the pilot," said a voice filled with worry over the radio. "Could you confirm there was supposed to be a skyscraper?"

"Pilot, confirmed. Why?" Dean looked at Ellie, who had no connection to the pilot's radio.

"Oh, you know, I just thought I'd waste your time. Oh no wait, *it's bloody gone*!" The pilot activated the red light and opened the door with a flick of a button.

Dean got up from his seat and looked out the door. He was attached to the roof of the metal death trap by a wire and clip, which didn't let him far onto the ramp, but just far enough to lean.

The skyscraper was on its side in hundreds of pieces. Dean looked around but all he could see was rubble and debris. Nothing was moving. There were no clouds of dust and no single speck of life.

A market plaza had been absolutely ruined, the statue of the founding lady turned to rubble, her head covered in the blood of the corpses littering the concrete.

"Right... you see that plaza?" Dean said into the radio. "That's where I want off. I don't want to head to the outskirts and put our backs against the walls".

He sat down and the door closed, leaving them all bathed in red light.

"Dean, what's up?" Ellie clicked her radio as she looked Dean in the eyes.

"I have a strong feeling that we don't want to be out in the open come nightfall," Dean clicked his own radio.

"Dean. Draxon said that to us that the first time we were down. Could they have really evolved since then?"

Everyone else was hanging on every word of their conversation.

The craft shook as it approached the landing, which made Ellie click her tongue in disappointment.

Dean said, "As far as we know, they evolved enough to make Verantians evolve and devolve. Who's to say they can't evolve further themselves, or even the other way round?" Dean clicked his radio off as the WarHawk began to suffer more turbulence.

The rear ramp opened just before touchdown and everyone got off quickly, Dean pushing the large ammo box, the conveyor of the WarHawk easing the load.

Dean clicked his radio. "Hey, do me a favour – head south of us and play some music or something really loudly through your speakers. Report if you see any movement."

The pilot lifted off, heading south, playing some old

Earth music – something to do with a fortunate son.

"Right, everyone, listen up," Dean called.

"Take eight extra mags each from this box and put them in a bag, which are also in the box. Asmodeus, take the weapon from the bottom – it's your sort of thing. If you need to hand off your current one, hand it to Ju Lan. We have approximately two hours till nightfall. Let's head for a building and stay quiet, we don't want to be caught moving at night. You have fifteen minutes – let's go." Dean loaded up his own bag then stepped back to cover for the others.

After fifteen minutes they left the ammo box to head further into the city, towards the fourth city gate. Almost an hour later, they found a wine shop with a basement, which they hid in for the rest of the night. They had been jogging since they set off from the landing site. They had searched every still intact building along the way but only the winery had a big enough basement for everyone.

Dean retreated to one corner with Ellie and Ju Lan. They slept next to him, their heads resting on his shoulder.

Many of the others looked at Dean jealously, but the smart ones took no notice, far too busy making sure they weren't jumped by anything.

"Lieutenant Colonel," said one of the female soldiers as she approached Dean. She was shaking from head to toe and flinched at everything. Her own shadow caused her much grief as it danced in the torchlight.

"What can I do for you, Lance-Corporal?" Dean kept his voice at a whisper.

The Lance-Corporal followed suit. "Sir... how do you do it? Remain so calm?" She was shaking so much the laser sight on her rifle bounced between the floor and Dean's eyes.

Dean pulled his arm out from behind Ju Lan's back and reached forward, holding onto the rifle barrel to keep the red light from hitting his eyes.

"What's your name?" he asked.

Jane let Dean guide the barrel of her rifle to the floor. "Jane Langley... from Earth... London."

"Well, Jane, unfortunately I cannot help you. I'm quaking in my boots, just like you. The difference is I have friends I've let down countless times already. By showing my fear physically, I would not only let them down, but all of you as well. So please feel free to show your fear. Make sergeant and you'll have to confine your fear. When you have people to protect that's the only fear you can have time for – whether or not they're going home." He put his arm behind Ju Lan's back again and she moved closer to him.

"Yes sir." Jane bit her lip. "One more thing..."

"Yes?" Dean smiled and laughed as Ellie moved closer, her hair tickling his nose.

"How did you do it?" She indicated the girls. "How did you get two pretty girls this dedicated to you?"

The jealous cadets around them were hanging onto the conversation like a lifeline. That stopped when the hatch opened and Asmodeus came in, shaking his head in boredom.

"You know… I don't know," Dean said with a smile.

Jane got to her feet, walking over to the stairs.

"It's your personality, moron," Ellie murmured without opening her eyes.

#

As the night passed the screams of the dead could be heard as they tore through the city. The WarHawk had long since left, but some of the human cadets were still muttering the song it had been playing. The cadets had all become jumpy, fearing closing their eyes.

Dean watched everyone until his watch beeped, telling him it was now day.

"Alright, everyone," he said, "I need two volunteers to walk slightly ahead of the pack. I'll be at the front while the rest of you will stick together. These things are no longer living, but there is an intelligence to them." As he stood up, the girls got up too, both yawning, looking well rested compared to the rest of them.

One of the male cadets stepped forward. "Shouldn't we all be in the group? Safety in numbers and all that?"

A thin layer of dust had settled overnight, covering everyone at least a little. One of the boys who had hidden behind the wine barrels came crawling out with red eyes and a red face from crying.

"Actually we should, but we can't afford to," Dean replied. "The group needs to protect our engineer, and the two at the front are there to keep them from surrounding the group by moving externally. I will keep the dead away from those two, at my own risk. Also, safety in numbers doesn't apply when the entire city is trying to kill you."

He cocked his rifle and went up the wooden ladder, peeking out of the basement hatch before moving all the way out.

The group slowly moved closer to the wall of the city. When they reached it, the engineer plugged a tablet into an access port. She had been working carefully for ten minutes when the tablet shorted out. She soon got it working again, but a look of horror appeared on her face, as all the settings had reverted to the previous ones that had been saved, a few hours into the night.

In an instant it became night again, a dark night with no moon or stars. People began to panic.

"Everybody, calm down," Dean ordered. "Put on your torches and keep your eyes open."

His own torch was much brighter than the others, but still they were blanketed in darkness, as if they were standing in the shadow of a thousand giants.

All anyone could hear was heavy breathing. The torch lights scanned for movement. Nobody so much as shuffled their feet. They stayed as still as they could, surrounding the engineer like a wall of flesh. The engineer confirmed the lock and unplugged her tablet.

The day returned, but it was too late.

Zombies rushed the group and everyone opened fire. The firefight lasted a few seconds and then night fell once more. The short out had clearly infected the system and was now playing havoc with the advanced yet sensitive settings of the habitat dome.

Everyone continued firing until day returned or the zombies were gone, no one really knew which one came first.

The day-night cycle was now completely messed up, leaving it early dawn before the group gathered themselves.

Eventually, the engineer reined it in and the day returned, a little duller than before.

The soldiers looked around happily, but Dean wasn't celebrating. One rifle was on the ground, accompanied by an LMG, both with blood on them. Their owners were gone.

He looked around for the bodies but couldn't see them.

Ellie and Ju Lan were gone.

#

"Friends won and lost make up the only reason soldiers fight on. They fight not for gravel or dust. Not for ideologies forced upon them. But for the bond with those around them."

– Draxon Black, *Notes for Dean*

Chapter Twelve: One Mission Now Two

Dean quickly began to lose his mind. His hands, arms, legs, and toes began to shake and air became hard to take in. He looked around again and again, desperate for a glimpse of them.

"Ellie! Ju! Ellie! Ju! Where are you?" he called, over and over. The rest of the group watched him in his madness as he searched.

"Sir, sir – Dean!" Jane grabbed him by the arms and held him still. He was sweating and crying and he'd turned so white you'd think had died on the spot.

"We need to finish the mission, Dean," Asmodeus said, putting a hand on Dean's shoulder. The snake man's hand was heavy. It refocused Dean, turning him back into some form of a leader.

"Yes. The mission... the mission. You must finish the mission." Dean began to walk off, but Asmodeus got in his way.

"What do you mean, 'you'? It's *we*, Dean." Asmodeus towered over Dean, watching the young boy, who sighed and looked up at Asmodeus's snake-like face.

"I can't... I need to find them. You guys need to get the mission done, then get out. I'll be fine... I won't let them turn into my brother... I won't keep running."

Dean broke out of Asmodeus's grip and walked off.

He passed the city, looking everywhere, following every blood trail.

That's when he realised exactly where he was.

He was standing exactly where he had been when the boy had spoken to him – the boy surrounded by zombies.

The buildings that had once surrounded the crossroads were now rubble. Beneath them were fleshless bones, and just ahead Dean could even make out a makeshift camp with skeletons strewn about.

The crossroads themselves were maintained, as if someone had purposefully moved the heavy debris out of the way to form a makeshift wall around the crossroads.

"Show yourself! Give me my friends back!" Dean yelled.

To his surprise, he got a response: a small zombie girl who came crawling out of the rubble holding a piece of paper. She handed it to Dean.

Dean uncrumpled the note. On it was written in blood the word *sewers*. The blood was relatively fresh.

"Sewers? Is this where my friends are?"

The girl pointed to an open manhole cover in the centre of the next intersection. She managed to croak the word, "Waiting..." before running off, screaming, slithering under a pile of rubble to watch Dean from the darkness.

Dean pocketed the paper and approached the drain.

He descended the ladder into the dark depths of the fifth city sewers. On the way down he slipped, his hands covered in blood from the ladder.

He fell onto his back, which broke him out of his panicked frenzy. Now clear-headed and focused, he realised the challenge he had taken on alone.

The sewers were large, dimly lit tunnels that created a labyrinth under the city. Each city had their own set of sewers and they all headed to the same place. The fifth city sewers were fairly well maintained and were clearly meant for more than just the occasional worker. Dean didn't smell the normal smell he associated with the sewers they were building on the new Verantian homeworld. It was a different smell. The smell of death, rotten flesh and rat droppings.

He stopped walking as his radio clicked.

"Dean. This is Draxon. Asmodeus told me you've gone off after Ellie and Ju Lan alone. Stop and tell me where you are. I'm coming down with a team. We can—"

Dean shut off his radio. He stood motionless for a few seconds. The last time he'd broken the rules in this way, he was punished with a punch. He chuckled and shook his head. A punch was the least of his worries.

He kept walking through the dirty, grimy sewers, eventually coming to a gathering of zombies.

He checked them all, but none of them were his friends, so he went to push on – but the zombies got in his way.

"Get out of my way!" Dean yelled, his voice echoing around the tunnels.

One of the zombies lifted his arm, pointing towards a small metal door that had been painted so that you might walk past it without a glance.

Dean pushed through it. The floor was wet and there were drag marks – not blood, but water. Large feet dragging two small sets of feet.

The interior was a bunker, obviously military in nature, and it contained many documents in boxes on shelves and on the floor. Dean took the time to scan through them, though he didn't know why he had stopped – in fact, he was fighting against the urge to look around, right up until he found an indicator as to the owner of the bunker.

Dead on the floor of a small room to one side were the corpses of six high-ranking Syndicate officers, all of whom had been eaten or eaten each other.

He shut the door on them and sighed loudly. Then he heard a shuffling sound through the next door. Slowly, he made his way over, his finger on the trigger of his rifle. He reached forward and opened the door to reveal a long, dim corridor with flickering lights and a dripping pipe.

At the end of the corridor was another door and standing outside it was Travis, the dead soldier who had been with Ellie and Ju Lan when they had landed the first time.

Travis had once been as well-built as Draxon, and his dark skin had set him aside from the others. Now he was a walking corpse, his clothes ripped, his face scratched and his chest torn open. His red eyes scanned Dean before acknowledging him.

"You took them, didn't you Travis?" Dean demanded. "You could easily drag them here. Are they alive?"

Travis nodded before pushing the door open. There was something very off about him in the way he looked at Dean with respect – or was it envy? Was Travis envious of Dean being alive? Very few of Dean's questions were about to get answers.

Dean entered a room littered with pipes and computers. Behind a mesh fence gate, tied to some pipes, were Ellie and Ju Lan. They were gagged and tied a foot away from a feral zombie chained to a pipe.

Sitting on a chair was the boy Dean had spoken to, who had warned him the first time.

"Hey there, soulless man," the boy said. "Tell me, was your bomb meant to kill all of us, or what?" He was severely burned but alive.

In his hand he held one of the shoes belonging to the little girl who had been blown up by Draxon.

Dean took off his rifle and put it on the ground. "My name is Dean. And I only came for my friends. Let them leave here alive, I beg you."

"No, *Dean*. You don't get to make the deal. Sorry. There's a side to me that comes out when I relax, you see. I'm all that stands between you and death – and I'm weakening. So tell me, Dean, what will happen when I die? How many of your friends will you lose? Ten? Twenty? You might save these two, but what about the others?"

The boy pointed to a camera monitor that showed Asmodeus and the others near the debris of the old tower.

"I just want these two," Dean said. "They're the only ones I care about. And if you want the person responsible for the girl's death, he's on his way... you can be sure of that."

Dean approached the mesh fence, but the boy raised a pistol. It was old and had been customised beyond need and it looked a little heavy for the boy, whose hand was shaking.

"I'd hate to have to pull the trigger," the boy said, "but I can't let you get them until your friends plug in to secure that door. Until I can sleep."

Dean looked the pistol over again and again, developing a plan.

"Fine. Fine," he said. "You win. Everyone I care about will die the moment you fall asleep or die. Then I'll be alone, just like you. But I have less to lose."

Dean pulled out his own pistol and pointed it at his own head.

The boy stared at Dean in confusion. "What are you doing?"

"You want me to suffer. But I won't. You kill either of my friends from that group or this one, and I die. No two ways about it."

Dean cocked the hammer of his pistol. He couldn't stop his hand from shaking. He couldn't help but think back to the shuttle, then to his brother, then to a blurred image of a bearded man smiling as a blade pierced his heart.

"Alright. What were you saying about the man who killed the girl?" The boy put down his pistol and Dean eased the hammer back into place.

Dean turned his radio on and clicked it. "Draxon. I'm in the sewers with someone who wants revenge. He's seen he can't make me suffer, so he intends to make *you* suffer. Fifteen or three. Sewers or the mission. Remember what you said to me – remember the phrase used by General Escinoriton before the battle of Deritorlorn. Remember *Numer'oos Esp'varni Lacari'nori Terani.*" Dean took off his radio and threw it aside.

The boy raised the pistol again. "What did you just do, Dean?"

"I just saved my friends. All of them."

He shot the feral zombie, then he shot Travis as he charged, knocking him into a concrete wall. Dean spat blood but lifted his pistol and shot Travis three times in the head.

The boy got up and started running. The zombies in the tunnels flooded towards Dean, who struggled to his feet, closing, and locking the door. He pulled the gate open and untied Ellie and Ju Lan.

"Dean, you're an idiot! I hate it when you do stupid stuff, you arsehole!" Ellie yelled whilst hugging him, and Ju Lan hugged the both of them.

"Okay, okay. Yell at me later. We need to find a way out of here."

Dean put them both on their feet, then picked up his rifle and gave it to Ellie.

"Dean! There are maps here. We can use them to find a way out..." Ju Lan pointed to a map on the wall of the old command centre. "Here!"

Dean nodded to her. He reloaded his pistol and gave it to Ju before taking the sword from his back, only to find it was chipped.

"That's not good. A chip... This was supposed to be unbreakable," Dean muttered as the girls were getting ready to leave.

They fought their way through what seemed an endless horde of zombies trapped in the next few rooms, but eventually made it out of the bunker and back into the large tunnels. Dean remained at the back, making sure no zombies came close to the girls, but during the gunfire he felt something hot and metallic graze the back of his head. He put his hand up to feel blood, and a wound that seemed to be pulsing. He wiped the blood from his sword with his hand, making sure the girls saw, both disgusted by it. Together, they made their way through the emptiest routes they could find, killing another hundred or so zombies between them, taking both girls to the last of their ammo before they arrived at the nearest ladder.

Just beyond the ladder was a large opening that led to many other tunnels – except water didn't flow out into the opening, but down into the opening, at least fifty feet down.

"Alright, you two head up first." Dean sent Ellie up the ladder and Ju Lan began to follow. As Ellie got the manhole open, a horde of zombies erupted from the many access holes and tackled Dean, pushing him over the waterfall they had navigated around.

"Dean – no..." Ellie watched as the horde kept running until had rushed over the side. Ellie didn't hear them hit the bottom, though she wasn't listening for that, or anything.

She and Ju Lan climbed back down and approached the edge slowly. As Ju Lan looked over it, Ellie broke down in tears. She knelt in the running water, looking into the pitch-black hole in despair. One of her only friends was gone forever.

"Ellie – come look!" Ju Lan called.

Ellie came running. Dean was just below them, on a metal-grate catwalk, along with three zombies. Ellie lifted the rifle and shot the zombies that were still moving, before jumping down with Ju Lan.

Dean was unconscious, but alive.

When he woke up, his head was resting on Ellie's lap and Ju Lan was asleep against her back. Dean could tell from the red rings around the girls' eyes that they'd been crying, and from the wrappers and a soaked-through, bloody bandage that someone had been hurt badly.

He coughed and tried to get up, but a sharp pain in his chest and stomach made him look down. His sword was snapped off – inside his own body. Every movement he made reopened the wound.

"Ah... fuck..." Dean gritted his teeth.

Ellie began to stroke his hair, her hand covered in blood. "You fucking idiot. Don't move... just relax." She didn't sound angry, only sad and tense.

"I'm sorry. I thought they might not come after me... but I was wrong. Looks like I'm no longer protected." Dean coughed up blood and Ellie wiped his mouth with her sleeve.

"Shh... shh... you need to rest. Just rest and wait." She continued to stroke Dean's hair, seeming to become more worried with every cough.

Ju Lan was looking at a blank concrete wall. "Ellie?" she said, "didn't your dad possess the power of fire?" An idea seemed to come to her as she clicked an old lighter.

"How does that help us now?" Ellie said bitterly.

"Didn't he burn one of Dean's wounds shut?" Ju Lan crawled around to look at Dean. The wound around the sword had opened slightly as he had tried to move, and he was now bleeding more heavily than before.

"Oh my god, you're right. Dean, you need to think about fire. As hot as you can imagine. Think about that heat in your hands as they make contact with something." Ellie grabbed Dean's hands and pressed one onto his wound.

Dean's hand quickly burned his flesh, sealing the exterior wound. The flame was bright and burned to look at. To

Dean it was only as though he was getting really badly sunburned.

"Okay, Dean, now think of something cold." Ellie put Dean's hand down.

Dean did as he was told, and the flame went away. Now he could breathe a little easier, but he was in even more pain and was deteriorating quickly. He was sweating and it was clear that his wounds, although now sealed, were infected. Without treatment, he would die, despite the healing prowess the Verantian people were known for.

Something heavy landed above them. Ellie grabbed the rifle and Ju Lan grabbed the pistol, both looking up to where footsteps could be heard. They were both shaking, soaking wet and cold. Dean, who was barely able to keep his eyes open, smiled.

The footsteps stopped just before the edge of the drop. The water that had been disturbed splashed on both girl's faces, stopping them from seeing properly.

Draxon's face peered over the edge of the waterfall. He sighed loudly. "Look at you three. Even in these circumstances, you're all still trying to sleep together."

He looked around before lying on his stomach and climbing down.

"Dean's seriously hurt," Ellie said. "We need to get him to the infirmary immediately."

Draxon reached into his backpack and pulled out a small blue bandage.

"This will be tight, Dean," he said, "but we need to keep that blade from moving." He wrapped the bandage around both Dean and the blade, then pulled it so tight that Dean could only just breathe.

"Draxon the boy took us hostage," Ellie said. "He used us to get to Dean because you killed that girl,"

Draxon nodded, as if he already knew. "I guessed that's what was happening from Dean's message. I have to get you guys out. This dome could come down on top of us."

He picked Dean up and jumped as high as he could, landing just above the waterfall, where he put Dean down and turned to help the others up.

"You girls go up first. I'll pass Dean up to you." Draxon let the girls climb the ladder before lifting Dean up. The girls were unable to get a grip due to their blood-covered hands, so Draxon and Dean struggled all the way up. There was blood on the side of Dean's head, which they hadn't noticed before.

"Draxon to WarHawk," Draxon said into his radio. "Pickup at LZ. I have wounded."

The WarHawk came soaring overhead, landing just

behind them in a clearing.

A horde of zombies, a mixture of men, women and children supported by various animals, all except for felines, charged out of the rubble and ruined streets, all heading for the WarHawk.

Draxon and the girls rushed over, putting Dean on a stretcher which had been on the ceiling of the WarHawk, tying him down as everyone else watched.

Draxon, Ellie and Ju Lan took their seats, Ellie sitting next to Dean, who fell unconscious shortly after take-off. The last thing he heard was that damn human song again.

Dean drifted in and out of consciousness several times, once on the WarHawk and twice in transit inside the Academy. The last time he awoke, he was on the operating table and a doctor was hurriedly cutting into his flesh, pulling out pieces of metal, poking around and cutting at his body. Dean wanted to move and scream but he couldn't – he could barely turn his head to see Ellie, who was watching with tears in her eyes. Then he fell unconscious once more.

Ellie watched as Dean was picked at by doctors like vultures picking at a corpse, or hyenas fighting over a long overdue meal. Ju Lan wasn't with her; Eren was worried about reinfection so she had been taken to the quarantine room for a twenty-four-hour quarantine.

Draxon was debriefing with Magnus and Asmodeus, and Eren was busy ordering cadets around to take her mind off Dean.

Everyone had become surprisingly fond of Dean, and him being in such a state almost brought the entire Academy to its knees. All lessons stopped, and for the three days Dean was under the scalpel, the entire academy respectfully and anxiously held its breath, simply hoping for the best.

Soon after the seventy-hour mark, the doctor came out of the operating room, completely covered in blood. He collapsed into a corner, just after he had told Magnus and Draxon that Dean was going to make it – just.

#

"To live beyond one's expectancy is impossible, for we decide before we are born when we die. We choose the time and the place and the exact details. Live in confidence that you didn't chose some pointless death."

– Draxon Black, *Notes for Dean*

Chapter Thirteen: Home for the Summer

Dean found himself dreaming of a figure in darkness. He'd dreamed of this man before. His mother called the man Ronlac. Dean's father. Dean felt closer to the man than to her, but he couldn't quite explain it.

He watched as the vision formed. Ronlac sat on the bridge of a ship. As people went about their business, he sipped on tea, winking as if he knew Dean was there. Then Dean saw his mother, younger by a few years but definitely her. She wore a full military outfit and was not pregnant, unlike the second woman next to Ronlac, who had pink eyes and a very beautiful dress.

Both girls received a gentle kiss from Ronlac, but Dean's mother seemed happier, for whatever reason.

Dean watched as they talked. There was no sound, but he was able to read their lips. His father was talking to the pregnant woman about names. He said he wanted it to be a strong name from the list of his ancestors, a name of the old Verantian monarchy that had built an empire in the stars.

The woman seemed less enthusiastic. She looked at Ronlac and just smiled. "I like the name Dean. I know it's human, but we can add it to Venurtari. Dean - Venurtari Ivanova. I like that."

Ronlac smiled in return and nodded.

Dean watched the vision for what felt like hours, until Ronloc said something – no sound coming from his mouth, only his lips moving. Then the vision shook and vanished.

The last words Dean had made out were shocking to him, and to the people of the vision.

Two hundred thousand.

Dean awoke in his room. His body was scarless and free of burns. He felt it all over, but all of his scars were gone. He looked around his room and grinned. Some gifts had been left for him at the foot of his bed, including a smart-looking watch and the many shards of the sword.

He walked around his room for a while, simply feeling the floor, the walls, the glass between him and space. He looked down at the gas giant that the colonies were built on. At first he experienced fear, but slowly he recovered his thoughts.

Sweat was dripping from his body, like water after having just got out of a pool. He walked into the bathroom and had a shower, which was hot – *very* hot. He laughed at the sensation. Steam filled the room and he embraced the concealment it gave. He let a few silent tears of relief and regret drip from his eyes before he pulled himself back into the present and his possible expulsion.

Coming out of the bathroom he took in the entire room.

The bed had been put back in with a new mattress that appeared a lot more comfortable than the last one. It still had hundreds of pillows, as the girls wanted, and it had the triple sleeping bag made from duvets. The computer desk had been extended and now contained three computers, and the plugs had extensions put in to handle the extra appliances and luxuries the girls used daily.

Thinking of the girls, Dean decided to check the drawers, the contents of which had been moved into three columns: one for Dean, one for Ellie and one for Ju Lan, from underwear to jackets.

The girl's dress uniforms were missing and the boots that Dean had spent an entire night polishing were also gone.

No one had come to see him. No girls. No Magnus. No Draxon. Dean was alone, and it freaked him out. He rushed to put on the bare minimum of clothing – a vest, trousers, and shoes – then ran from his room. He looked all over the Academy. He couldn't find anyone. He was alone.

He ran all the way around the Academy twice, in ever-increasing panic, but couldn't find anyone, not even the janitor. He had one more room to check – the room he had left till last in the hope they might be in there.

The empty Academy felt creepy. It was as if something was missing, something very important and so large in

Dean's heart that he could feel it skip every other beat.

Some of the corridors were completely dark, as if the Academy had been abandoned. In some places Dean thought he could see eyes, but after blinking they vanished. It was clear he had some sort of mental health issue, but he laughed about it before continuing his journey through the city station.

He slowed down as he went down the many stairs leading towards the hangar, his hand shaking the entire time and his footsteps echoing. With every step he took, he had an increasing urge to throw up, which he only suppressed by grabbing his throat.

For some reason, the elevators were not powered, and the corridors leading to the main auditorium and ranges were sealed shut. The massive, black, metal bulkhead doors thick enough to survive the biggest explosives were drawn across the corridor like heavy curtains.

When he opened the hangar doors, he was shocked and relieved at what he saw. The WarHawk was attached to the ceiling and the floor was filled with all the cadets, teachers and staff standing in parade formation, all in dress uniform.

As the door slid open they all saluted Dean. Draxon had even cleaned himself up and found himself a dress uniform that fit.

The Academy dress uniform was a crisp black fabric sewn with golden stitching and a white sash adorned with whatever medals and badges awarded to them, along with a hat with a golden phoenix on the front.

The girls had several medals and a few decent badges. Everyone had something, and the expressions on their faces made it clear they felt good about it. Those that had completed the colony mission Dean had led had all been awarded ranks, and the right to choose a weapon to specialise in, as represented by the badges pinned to their sashes.

Magnus stood at the very front, his own uniform white with gold trim. Ellie and Ju Lan stood behind him and the teachers surrounded the students. Like the others, they were all saluting Dean.

Dean approached slowly and uncertainly, saluting in response. He looked at Ellie, Magnus and Ju Lan, hoping for an explanation. Magnus had a scowl on his face. Though it was very slight, Magnus rarely frowned so it was as obvious as night and day.

"Dean Ivanova," a voice said from behind him. A man in very rich-looking robes with golden rings and gems lining his outfit approached, his footsteps silent. Dean noticed a badge in his hand.

"I'm confused..." Dean began.

"I suppose you are. Do you know who I am?" the man asked softly.

His short brown hair and beard were too neat for him to be a relative of Draxon, but Dean could feel the man's power.

"Before we get into some ceremony," Dean asked, "can I do something that's probably uncalled for?"

The man nodded and smiled.

Dean spun on his heel and barged past Magnus to hug both Ju Lan and Ellie, who hugged him back. All three of them let tears form.

Ellie tapped Dean's back. "Dean..."

He pulled away to look at her.

"I love you," he said. "Both of you. I'm never going to let something like that happen to you again – I can't bear to think where I'd be without you."

People laughed, but Ellie and Ju Lan both struggled to keep their tears back.

"Damn it, Dean... why'd you have to go and make me cry in front of the Emperor?" Ellie tried to dry her eyes, and Ju Lan turned away, using her sleeves to wipe her face.

"The Emperor? Why would he be here?" Dean said. "No, he's probably very far away in some palace, drinking the best wine with the best whores that money can buy, whilst his wife treats every child like her own... or something."

Dean laughed – but everyone else appeared mortified.

Draxon hit Dean hard on the back of the head and whispered in Dean's ear.

"Shit! I'm sorry – that was uncalled for. I meant no disrespect," Dean said in defence of his outburst. "We hear things, is all."

The Emperor laughed, and the other cadets and trainees laughed gently in the background, as Dean was shown up in front of the Emperor, wearing only his vest and trousers.

"Yes indeed, I am Emperor Xolistine the Second. I am here to award you with the highest honour a soldier in the empire can earn, and to do something... slightly out of character for me. And you weren't entirely wrong – I do enjoy expensive company."

Xolistine approached and took Dean's hand, shaking it. He handed Dean the badge and smiled.

"I thought I'd already achieved the highest rank?" Dean looked at the badge. The letters beneath it read CMNDR. It was slightly heavier to every other badge Dean had been given. Much like the others, it had the phoenix, but this one was shaped more like a shield, almost triangular. It was made of solid gold and platinum with silver engraving.

"Dean. You have now achieved the rank of Cadet Commander. In your first year you made us create a new rank. This is a very rare occasion, but you led a team down to a zombified city and you even executed your very own rescue mission. You saved every member of your team and their parents will thank you for it. I used my powers to heal your wounds and even paid someone else a visit before I came here." The Emperor indicated the formation of cadets, which split into two groups.

Dean's younger brother and mother stood at the back, both crying happily. Dean's brother was standing on his own two legs, without even a set of crutches. His mother looked ever so slightly older than in Dean's vision, but not drastically. She was a brunette with curly hair that looked like a bird's nest. She was wearing an old uniform that had a hole in it, and which looked like it had been ever so slightly extended around the waist, the leather belt on its third to last buckle, despite the fact that she wasn't a very big lady at all.

Dean was caught off guard. He had no clue what was happening, but his body moved for him. He sprinted along the hangar and leapt at his family, hugging them extremely tightly.

"I thought you guys hated me... it was all my fault," he said, about to break into tears.

His mother shook her head. His brother simply buried his head in Dean's chest, letting loose a torrent of tears that dropped to the floor like anchors.

"Your brother never blamed you for a second," his mother said. "I did... at first. But when you left nine months ago, I realised that whilst one of my sons had become crippled, I had forced my other son out... I'm so sorry, baby." She began to cry tears of regret.

"Why did you never write to me? Tell me this?" Dean said, annoyed. "To feel less hated would have been nice!"

"I wanted to, but you never actually told me where you were going. You even got up earlier than I did to get out without saying goodbye." Dean's mother was trying to hold it all back.

Everyone watched the family for a few minutes. The few people that had still disliked Dean now looked at him with understanding and slight regret.

"Dean, I would like to ask something of you," Magnus said as he walked over. His scowl was gone and a smile crept across his face like an insect.

"Anything, sir." Dean said with a salute.

Magnus chuckled and saluted back. "I would like you to come stay at my house over the summer at some point.

Your family is welcome, too. It's just..." Magnus leant to whisper in Dean's ear.

"It's just, with her father gone and her mother working all summer, I need someone to watch my granddaughter... Some of the stuff you said whilst unconscious gave me the impression you weren't going to let her leave your sight." He stood up straight.

Dean held out his hand. "It would be an honour, sir..."

As they shook hands, the cadets and teachers crowded around them.

"Everyone passed this year," Magnus said, "just so everyone knows... Paper packets and invites for next year will be sent out next week. Congratulations."

Everyone cheered. Amongst the crowd of teenagers, Dean's twelve-year-old brother jumped around, getting knocked over occasionally only to get right back up and jump like he'd never jumped before.

Ellie and Ju Lan approached Dean.

"So, Dean," Ellie said, being louder than Ju Lan for once. "You're coming to the house. That just leaves Ju Lan to invite."

Dean guided them out of the group so they could talk, the mess of teens in uniforms confusing enough to lose the star of the show, a princess, and their friend.

"Well, why don't you just invite her? In fact, if she

doesn't come I'll have to kidnap her, just to make sure she's safe."

Dean smiled at Ju Lan, who put her arm around Dean and Ellie, who did the same.

"How are you feeling Dean?" Ju Lan asked. "You had us really worried." She guided the trio to the hangar shield, which hummed quietly in the background like a bumblebee making its way from flower to flower.

"I'm perfectly fine. 'fraid you won't have any more scars to glide your fingers over, though."

Dean smiled, and the girls looked at each other, then linked their arms so they were in a small circle.

"You said you're keeping your eyes on us," Ellie said. "But we want to keep our eyes on you. I was thinking, and Ju Lan agreed, that Varantian law states that under certain circumstances Verantians can be betrothed from the age of fourteen. Both me and Ju Lan will be fourteen next month." She looked Dean in the eye.

In confusion, Dean said, "I'm sorry... Did you guys just jointly propose to me?" He took a step back.

Ellie and Ju Lan looked at him in concern.

"Is something wrong Dean?" Ju Lan asked.

Dean turned away. "Do you know how expensive having a joint wedding, or two weddings, will be? Our combined salaries won't be enough to cover my mother's taste in décor." Dean laughed.

The girls looked at one another.

"Did he just say yes?" Ellie asked Ju Lan. "Because I can't tell."

"I said yes, idiots. Come here."

Both girls jumped at him, knocking him to the ground.

"Did you guys hear that?" Draxon called out into the crowd. "Commander Ivanova just agreed to marry not one, but *two* girls under his command!"

Both Ellie and Ju Lan turned red.

Draxon was elbowed in the stomach by Eren, whilst Magnus held himself back from crying before getting out his tablet and slowly walking away.

"Yeah? What of it?" Dean leant in and kissed Ellie on the cheek, before kissing Ju Lan in the same way, sending both girls so red they made tomatoes look blue.

The Emperor approached from behind them, summoning a piece of paper from thin air and handing it to Dean.

"This is a personal reward from me for your amazing work, cadet."

As Dean looked down at the paper, Xolistine disappeared.

"He gave me a *ship*?"

Both Magnus and Draxon ran over to confirm it. At the same moment, a black and gold starship emerged from a white tunnel, entering orbit of the planet.

"That is the Mercy," Magnus said. "She's an old ship, but the most powerful of her size. A good reward, and very out of character." He patted Dean's back as everyone else left, leaving Dean, Ellie and Ju Lan staring out at Dean's new ship.

Dean looked over his shoulder at the lab and left the girls to approach to it. He touched the doors and they slid open. The interior hadn't been touched or cleaned out, and the prototype SMG was gathering dust on the desk.

"Dean?" Ellie said as she approached. Ju Lan came from the hangar too, removing her dress uniform.

"Next year, this room will be a gym on one side, a tinkering area on the other," Dean said. "You, me, Ju Lan and whoever becomes our teammates will be able to use it to our hearts' content". He walked deeper into the room then turned back around to the girls. "I meant it, by the way... I love you both. I've had friends before... even a girlfriend... but with you two, there's no comparison."

As Dean walked out of the room he tripped slightly, and Ellie caught him.

"You know running a ship is more expensive than two royal weddings, right?" she said as she helped him across the hangar.

"I'm just going to have your grandfather look after it for me... at least until I graduate." Dean's leg had fallen completely asleep, so he and Ellie were forced to limp back to their room. "Hey," he added, "so, about me visiting over the summer... would it be alright for me to visit from start to finish?" He pointed to a bench on the floor above the hangar, where they could take a quick rest.

"I'd love to, but you'd be alone for the first three quarters. My mum will be away working and my grandma on my mother's side would like me to meet the other fourteen cousins..." Ellie rested her head back. "Gah, Christmas is going to be so expensive this year. I don't even celebrate it!"

Dean laughed, lifting his sleeping leg and wiggling his big toe. "Fourteen cousins... I have one cousin and she starts next year. Oh god, is my brother coming too? Crap, this summer is going to suck... well, the first three quarters of it." Dean rested his head back as well.

Sitting there on the bench, they both fell asleep, Dean

still thumbing his new badge and Ellie with her head on his shoulder.

As everyone had been told, they had all passed. But when it came time to leave, there was an extra ship: a small quarantine shuttle with crew wearing heavy looking, metal reinforced, armour.

Dean's shuttle was waiting for its pilot before it could leave. In the meantime, Dean looked out the window at the small shuttle. He couldn't believe what he saw. Danny and Danni, healed and perfectly fine, were walking in cuffs. Danni was heavily pregnant.

Dean pushed himself up against the glass, but before he could get a better look, the shuttle launched. He looked around to see that Ju Lan and Ellie were asleep in their bunks.

The two human boys they had initially travelled with had begun an arm-wrestling tournament. Dean resumed staring back into space.

"To end the story at the beginning is lazy writing. To write a tale that has no meaning is poor craftsmanship. To expect money for nothing is pure greed and selfishness. We have planned our stories to be told and all our lives have meaning. Whether we have money or things is not true wealth. Our wealth comes from those around us, right down to the ants we spare."

– Magnus Phoenix, *Phoenix Academy Handbook*

END

Printed in Great Britain
by Amazon

60751195R00137